The Naive Wife

Rachel's Choice

UFUOMAEE

THE NAIVE WIFE: RACHEL'S CHOICE

Copyright © 2019 Ufuomaee

2020 Edition

All rights reserved.

ISBN: 9781689165655

This novel is a work of fiction. The names, characters and incidents portrayed in it are the work of the author's imagination. Any resemblance to actual persons, living or dead, events or localities is entirely coincidental.

Photo credit: www.pixabay.com
Unless otherwise stated, all Scriptures referenced are from www.blueletterbible.org.

All rights reserved. No part of this book may be reproduced, stored in a retrieval system, transmitted in any form or by any means-electronic, mechanical, photocopying, recording, or otherwise-without prior permission in writing from the copyright holder.

DEDICATION

"Trust in the LORD with all thine heart; and lean not unto thine own understanding. In all thy ways acknowledge him, and he shall direct thy paths" (Proverbs 3:5-6).

To our God, who is able to lead all His children and preserves them in all their troubles. And to the ones who trust in Him, come what may.

AUTHOR REVIEWS

"You constantly allow God use you to correct the misinformation and vices in our world today and you do it in such a way that everyone gets the point. You really are amazing!"
- *Ifeoluwapo Alatishe* -

"Ufuomaee is a realist (I love the fact that she includes happenings in the society in her stories, sensitive topics we don't like to talk about. For instance, of sexual abuse in the Church and home as portrayed in The Church Girl and Broken respectively). Ufuomaee has that magical power to keep her readers spellbound. I also love the fact that she writes from a Christian perspective."
- *Jesutomilola Lasehinde* -

"Truly, you are one of the few people I delight in reading their posts. You make the book so real, I sometimes see myself as one of the characters. And I've been blessed by your books. You have a unique style of portraying your characters. You give them life."
- *Folashade Oguntoyinbo* -

"Ufuomaee is an author that writes fiction as though it is real. A Christian not ashamed to put her values into writing and I find myself reading the Bible passages she puts at the beginning of her stories. A great author whom everyone needs to read from."
- *Jimi Kate Darasimi* -

ACKNOWLEDGMENTS

To my Father in Heaven; for being my muse, my counsellor, and my strength. To my father on Earth; for doing your very best for me. To my mom; for your sacrifices and unconditional love. To my husband; for choosing me and supporting me in this ministry. To Ijeoma; for your editorial input and advice on this project. To my readers; for your feedback, encouragement, and prayers!

THANK YOU!.

CHAPTER ONE

"Hey, it's a beautiful, sunny Friday. What are you doing? I'm Rachel Eden, and I'm your host on Love Lounge on 94.2 Urban FM until 4 pm. Our question today is "How Do You Know When It's Love?" Our lines are open, and I'm here for you... Holla!"

The lines light up, and Rachel smiles at her producer before pressing the button to take the caller on line 1. "Hi, Caller... Where are you calling from?"

"Hi, Rachel! I love your show! I'm Foluke from Lagos Island."

"Thanks for calling in, Foluke. Are you single, dating, or married?"

"I'm engaged! He proposed last night!"

"Oh, wow... Con-gra-tulations!!! So, how do you know when it's love?"

"It's the absence of fear... It's freedom. I just know that Jide is the one because I've never been so happy in my life. I just...I can't wait to marry him!"

"We're all happy for you here. And I love your answer... *The absence of fear!* The Bible says that *"Perfect love casts out all fear"*, so I feel you! Foluke, do you have a song request?"

"Yes, please. This is dedicated to you, Jide... "If I Ain't

Got You" by Alicia Keys."

"Coming right up! Thanks for calling in. Many congratulations to Jide and Foluke who have found love in each other. It's so sweet when you find what you've been searching for your whole life. You guys are an inspiration to those of us still looking and hoping!"

Alicia Keys sings in the background softly, and Rachel disconnects her microphone so that the song is playing loudly in the air waves. She closes her eyes as she listens to the lyrics of the song. When will she ever feel that way about somebody? She lets out a deep sigh.

"That was Alicia Keys, "If I Ain't Got You", requested by Foluke from Lagos Island," Rachel says, after the song plays out. "Our question remains "How Do You Know When It's Love?" Caller on line two, where are you calling from?"

"Hi, Rachel, good afternoon. This is Innocent."

"Hello, Innocent. Thanks for calling. Where you at?"

"I'm in Maryland, Ikeja. And I love you."

Rachel blushes, despite the regularity of such sentiments expressed by her callers; male and female. "So, I have to ask: How do you know when it's love?"

In a husky, low voice, Innocent answers, "When you think about her all the time. When you dream about her too. When her voice ignites your world, and her joy and safety is your utmost concern."

"Hmmm... Deep! Are you a poet?"

"I'm just a lover... And I got it bad... For you!"

Rachel steals a glance at her producer. He is indicating that she cut off the call as soon as she can, by sliding his hand across his neck sharply, a serious expression on his face.

"Alrighty then! Thanks for calling. Do you have a song request?"

"Usher. "U Got It Bad". Take care, Rachel Eden."

Rachel swallows, even as she puts his song request on. He's not the first caller to make her the object of his love, and she knows it's an expected inconvenience of her career as a radio talk show host. But even though it's flattering, it isn't always fun.

Taking her headphones off, she looks at Dongjap, her producer. Her ever protective boss. He's looking in her eyes as he asks, "You alright?"

She shrugs. "I'm cool."

***

"That was a good show today," Dongjap says.

"Thanks," Rachel beams. "Friday is always the best."

Dongjap smiles. "Everyone's preparing for the weekend, that's why. Any plans?"

Rachel shrugs. "You know me… I've got choir practice tomorrow, before I come in for my shift."

Dongjap nods. "Yeah, I know… I wish you'd do something different, though."

She chuckles. "Yeah, right. What you up to?"

"Out with the guys tomorrow night. Bday things. You should join us." He looks at her, watching as she tucks away a strand of curly weavon from her caramel-toned face. Flawless beauty. Her full pink lips catch his eyes as she sucks the bottom lip in briefly to moisten it. She does that too often. Doesn't she know the effect it has on him? He swallows.

Rachel laughs. "Not a chance, Dj. You know I don't do the night thing. But you guys should have fun!"

She goes to hug him. "Happy birthday in advance!"

Dongjap receives her in a tight embrace, not able to stop himself from taking in her scent. *Fruity. And a touch of Aloe vera.* He releases her. "See you tomorrow…"

"Aight…" she says, as she leaves the studio, without a glance back. She wants to make it home in time to study.

In addition to hosting her own radio show, serving and singing in Church, and volunteering with a children's charity, Rachel's taking an online course on Counselling, with a focus on Marriage and Relationships. She'd always wanted to become a Marriage Counsellor, and has been regarded as a bit of a relationship expert, even though she'd only ever had one serious relationship in her life. Everyone she knows seeks her out whenever they have issues in their relationships, and her radio show has given her a platform to reach so many more people in need of marital and emotional guidance. Taking the course was a decision she made, not only to advance her career but, to protect those who trusted her for wise, godly counsel.

On getting to her car in the parking lot, she stops at the shout of her name. Turning in the direction of the call, she sees Seun Emmanuel approach her hastily. "Please, can you drop me at CMS?"

Rachel should have known to wait for her. It's been the same request every Friday evening, since she took on the new position at Urban FM. She smiles at her friend and colleague.

"Sure…" she says, knowing she might end up going all the way to Seun's house at Obalende. Whenever the traffic isn't too bad, she often makes that detour. She is fortunate to have a car, and she understands that not many people in Lagos are as fortunate as she.

***

"So, any plans for the weekend?" Rachel asks casually, as she drives fast on the Surulere bridge. The traffic at this time is not too bad, and she should be at CMS in less than ten minutes.

Seun shrugs. "Not really."

Hmmm… Rachel ponders. Should she prod or just enjoy the silence? She decides not to, as a cool breeze rushes into the car. She smiles with nostalgia.

"Do you?"

Rachel turns at Seun's question, saved from dredging up feelings from an old romance. "Yeah, not much…"

"I bet you're going for Dj's hangout."

"Actually, no. Not my kinda thing. You going?"

"I wish! But he never invited me. I heard he only invited a couple of girls, and only the on-air personalities." Seun twists her mouth into a frown as she eyes Rachel from the side. No doubt, she was invited. "Let's go together, nau... It will be fun!"

"Seriously, aside being totally over the whole clubbing scene, I've got so much reading to catch up on for my course. I'm sorry, I can't. But you should go, nau... I'm sure he wouldn't mind."

"You think?"

"Yeah! Dj's real cool."

Seun beams, hopeful. "Thanks. You don't think it's too...*desperate*?"

Rachel turns to give Seun a quick glance, before returning her eyes to the road. "Hmmm... You like him, don't you?"

Seun blushes. "Who doesn't? He's so dreamy..."

Hmmm, Rachel contemplates. She'd noticed his good looks but never allowed herself to consider him beyond that since he was, clearly, an irreligious man. She knew the type of man she was looking for, and Dongjap wasn't him.

She knew he liked her, though. She often caught him staring, and she was definitely flattered, but she couldn't waste her time dating because of attraction. The next man had to be the last man, so it was only friendship she offered him. And so far, it was working fine.

She shrugs. "He's cute. I suppose."

"Cute?!" Seun chuckles. "He's so fine and rugged, he puts Method Man to shame! Anyway... I actually thought there was something going on between you two..."

They arrive at CMS Bus stop, where Rachel slows down for Seun to alight.

Rachel swallows and shakes her head. She doesn't feel like going to Obalende tonight. She's not sure she can handle much more of Seun's talk about Dj.

Seun removes her seatbelt and gathers her things. "Well, that's good to know. Thanks for the lift, Rache!"

"Have a good weekend," she calls out, before pulling away and speeding off on the highway home. Thank God for some peace and quiet.

But with the peace and quiet come the nostalgic thoughts her mind longs to return to and linger on. The time of an almost happily ever after. The reason that, at 31 years old, she is still single. It had been so perfect. Well, almost.

Onyeka was a Christian. Actually, a Catholic. Back then, it was enough. They both believed in Jesus, as the Son of God. He was their Lord and Saviour, so the details of their worship and religion didn't matter. Plus, he was dreamy. Not Dj dreamy. *Blair Underwood* dreamy! God, his smile could stop traffic!

They were 29 years old when they met, and they both knew they were attracted to each other. Things moved pretty fast. After their third date, he'd asked for her blood type, because he was AS, and he'd previously had to end relationships that got deep, which had been too painful for him. He was overjoyed to learn that she was AA. It seemed like the confirmation they needed that they were meant to be.

Every conversation soon became about their marriage; the life they would live, how many kids they'd have, where they would live, and the holidays they'd take. They never even thought to explore their Faith and grow their relationships with God.

Things soon became carnal, and it all went downhill the first time they had sex. He'd convinced her that it was okay because they knew they were going to get married. And their love was special. Their passion was hot, and God would understand.

But God didn't understand. The guilt she felt was unbearable, as God called to her as He did Adam and Eve in the garden when they'd sinned. She started to see that their relationship was not about Him, but about her. About Onyeka. It was built on lust and not real love and, without Him as the cornerstone, it would surely crumble.

Rachel tried to withdraw, but Onyeka wouldn't let her. He said they wouldn't do it anymore, since she felt so bad about it. He rather proposed, and even with doubt in her heart, she accepted. But his parents did not approve. She wasn't Catholic!

In Romeo and Juliet style, he came after her. And she fell one more time for the profession of his lips. His parents would change their minds, once they got to know her and realised how crazy in love he was with her. But joy evaded her. She had no peace, until she hung their love on the Cross and walked away.

It was the hardest thing she had ever done. But it was the road to redemption and a deeper love with God than she'd previously known. Onyeka was not the one. God had someone better. He had promised, and she would believe.

Rachel wipes tears from her eyes as she parks in her parents' driveway, in Osborne Estate, Ikoyi. "Lord, I know You are enough for me, but please, I want my Adam. Please bring me someone to love…" she prays her usual plea. "In Jesus' name, amen!"

Stepping out of the car, she beholds the mansion she'd grown up in. The gardener is at work adding new plants and trimming the shrubs. Their home is getting a make-over, inside and out, to become the venue for her sister's marriage introduction next weekend.

Rachel smiles. She is happy for her sister. Sure, Rochelle is five years younger, but the race isn't to the swift. And it isn't a race, anyway.

It's not a competition. I'm happy for Rochelle.

CHAPTER TWO

The sequins on her African golden, lace blouse and wrapper shine, as Rochelle twirls in front of the ceiling-to-floor mirror, in her mother's room. Rachel admires her sister's natural long locks, which fall down to the middle of her back. She'd always envied her sister this trait she inherited from her mother, a beautiful Hausa woman.

But their likeness ended with their remarkable facial features; slim pointy nose, big wide eyes, high cheek-bones, deep-set dimples and small, rosy lips. Unlike the slender Mrs Eden, Rochelle was short and plump. Some might say chubby or fat but, to Rochelle, she is simply 'bootilicious'.

"Go and get the beads I laid out," comes Mrs Eden's instruction, as she approaches her daughter, who is still admiring her reflection in the mirror.

It is clear to Rachel that she's being spoken to, even if her step-mother does not address her by name. Today, her eyes are only for her precious daughter, whose fiancé is about to meet the family, in an official introduction, as per her father's tradition. The coral beads have been enhanced with diamonds, and the set looks good enough for a queen. When Mrs Eden places them on her daughter's ears, neck and wrists, and steps back to admire the bride, tears glisten in her eyes.

"Beautiful!" she says with emotion. "Come, let's take our photo before you go downstairs."

Rachel stands aside as the bride and her mother are photographed in different poses. The photographer invites her into the shot, and she goes to stand beside her sister. Mrs Eden is distracted and moves away as soon as the photographer has taken his shot. Rochelle continues to pose, and the photographer takes a few more shots of the sisters, before Mrs Eden cuts in and asks them to hurry up, as the groom and the elders have met and are now waiting for the bride.

***

Ekene Okafor looks up as his bride descends the stairs to the living area, where he is sitting with his parents, uncles and aunties. He has just expressed his interest in marrying one of the Eden daughters, pretending as if he had only just met her, as the traditional role play dictates. He'd told an elaborate story of how he saw her at the market and, upon exchanging words with her briefly, he knew he wanted to take her for his wife, and was now here to do the honourable thing.

He smiles as he recalls the truth. They hadn't met anywhere so innocent. The day he'd noticed her, she'd actually been 'dropping it like it's hot' at a club he frequented. He'd been watching her twerk her rounded, fat behind for at least ten minutes, before he'd decided to ask her to dance. She was out with her girlfriends, and they seemed to be having a twerking competition, as they bounced their butts to the music and laughed out loud. She won in his eyes.

"Is that her sister?!" his older brother, Ejike, asks, his eyes wide as he takes in Rachel, who's dressed simply in an ankara print dress. Her weave is packed up in a stylish bun, and her make-up is light, compared to the full mask the bride is wearing and, yet, she is stunning.

"Don't think about it, mehn!" Ekene whispers.

Ejike swallows, his eyes following Rachel as she enters the kitchen. "What's wrong with her?"

"She's not your type, trust me!"

"Virgin?"

"Worse. Born again virgin!"

"Oh… But still."

"Believe me… Don't waste your time."

***

Rachel twirls the old, gold chain her late mother had given her as a child. It is the only thing she still has of her birth mom, who'd passed away when she was just eight years old. Until then, she hadn't known that her mother was a kept woman, nor that her father had a whole other family in Lagos. It had been a rude awakening for Mrs Eden too, when Mr Eden had brought her into their home 24 years ago. Their boys, Ryan and Richard were twelve and ten years old, respectively, and Rochelle was just three years old. It had been hard, but they'd all done their best to make good of a bad situation.

Mrs Eden was no wicked step-mother, but despite her best efforts, she and Rachel remained distant. Rachel often felt Mrs Eden did just enough to include her, giving the impression of a happy family. Rachel was understanding and sympathetic to her step-mom, knowing that it couldn't have been easy for her to accept and adjust to the reality of her existence. She knew that every time Mrs Eden looked at her, she saw her mother, to whom Rachel bore a striking resemblance. At times when she felt cheated or neglected, Rachel consoled herself in the knowledge that Mrs Eden had done more for her than others would have, and she was grateful for that good fortune.

Rachel watches as the introduction ceremony continues with the arrival of her sister, the bride. Her brothers were not able to attend as they both now lived in the US. They'd be home in a couple of months, however, for the traditional and white wedding ceremonies. Rachel sighs, thinking how much she misses them, especially Richard, to whom she is closest. With them gone, she'd felt more like the odd one out, as Rochelle and Mrs Eden stuck together like twins. When Rochelle started dating Ekene, just six months ago, they became thick as thieves, as they plotted and planned every step to get to this day.

Rachel feels the heat of a pair of eyes on her and turns in the direction of the stare, just as Ejike looks away. She looks him over, figuring that he's the brother of the groom. He is quite handsome, she thinks. *I wonder if he's anything like his brother.* She smiles when he turns his gaze to her again. He returns a brilliant, white smile, and she looks away.

Rochelle is turning to leave, and Rachel quickly follows behind her. The bride's part of the ceremony is done. Now, it's time to change and eat a late lunch.

"Oh, I'm starving!" Rochelle groans, when they are back in her mother's quarters.

"Yeah, me too," Rachel concurs.

"Did you see the way Ejike was looking at you?" Rochelle asks, giggling. "As if you were on the menu, and he hasn't eaten in days!"

"Oh, who's that?"

"Ekene's brother. He was sitting beside him. He's doing a PHD in Port Harcourt. Do you think he's cute?"

Rachel shrugs. "He's attractive."

"Be careful, sha. He has a reputation, if you know what I mean…"

Rachel nods. "Yeah, I figured." She sighs.

The servant girl enters the room with a tray for the bride and sets it on the dining table. Rachel watches as she begins to leave. "Please bring me…"

"Madam say make you go kitchen, come collect your own…" the girl interrupts, speaking in broken English, as she continues to head out.

Rachel raises a brow at the rudeness and decides to say nothing. Rochelle's serving herself fried rice from a dish and paying no mind. "I'm going downstairs," Rachel says, feebly.

There's no response.

***

Downstairs, Rachel serves herself a plate of jollof rice, dodo and chicken, and takes her plate to the dining area to eat. She notices that some of the guests are still eating in the living area. Her father is sitting among them and, when he notices her sitting by herself, beckons her to come and meet their soon to be relatives.

"You are beautiful!" the father of the groom exclaims, when Chief Eden introduces his first daughter. "Have you met Ejike, my first son?"

Rachel simply smiles and curtsies. She greets all the uncles and the aunties, ignoring the ignorant comments of those who think she's the 'yellow' version of Mrs Eden, because she's closer to her in stature than her own daughter. It doesn't help that the only features she'd inherited from her father were her full lips, smile, and Nubian nose.

Ejike is unfortunately absent, and they are not introduced at this time. He must have gone outside with Ekene, Rachel assumes. She returns to her seat to finish her meal, eager for the day to be over and to make herself scarce.

"May I join you?"

Rachel looks up at the sound of that husky voice. Her heart beats in anticipation, as she expects to see a familiar face. But the voice belongs to an absolute stranger. She smiles wearily at him.

"Hi… Sure."

He stretches out a hand and introduces himself. "Hi, I'm Doug. You must be Rachel…"

She nods and takes his hand to shake it. He's not bad looking. Who is he?

"I'm Ejike's friend, in case you're wondering. Actually,

we're family friends. We're practically brothers," he smiles. He has a nice smile, she thinks.

"Have you eaten?" she decides to ask, remembering she's still a host for today.

Doug nods. "Yes, but I wouldn't mind some more chicken."

"Sure..." Rachel rises to go to the kitchen to get him a plate.

She returns to find Ejike seated at the table, next to Doug. Their eyes meet again, and he gives her his dashing smile. Heat rushes to her cheeks as she blushes. *There's definitely something about him...*

"I don't think we've been introduced," he rises up, extending a hand, his eyes intent on her face. "I'm Ejike, Ekene's brother."

She drops the plate of chicken in front of Doug and smiles, receiving Ejike's hand. "I'm Rachel."

"Nice to meet you," they say together, and then giggle.

Rachel takes her seat again. At this point, her appetite has almost gone. She pushes her plate away, losing interest in the meal.

"Are you off somewhere?" Ejike asks, unable to hide the disappointment from his tone.

"Yeah..."

"Why, nau? Stay and chat with us!" Doug insists.

Rachel pauses and contemplates. It is less awkward chatting with both guys, instead of just one of them. She shrugs. "Okay."

"Great!" Ejike beams.

***

"So, you're Rachel Eden of Urban FM! Wow, I love your show!" Doug proclaims, after Rachel tells him why her voice sounds so familiar.

"I live in Port Harcourt, so I've never heard your show. Do you stream?" Ejike asks.

"Not all the shows. But a few."

"Okay… You should stream on YouTube. A lot of people are doing it these days," Ejike continues.

"Yeah, I've thought about it. But I still love the anonymity of being a radio celebrity."

"I see. I guess."

"So, do you have a boyfriend?" Doug asks, his gaze intent.

Rachel shakes her head. "No."

Doug smiles, and Rachel notices Ejike light up too. "What, are all the men around you blind or something?" Doug continues.

Rachel shrugs. "I'm just waiting on the right guy."

Ejike nods. "A Christian?"

Rachel looks in his eyes. "Yes… But not by name only."

Ejike sees the challenge in her eyes. He understands quite well what "not by name only" means. No doubt, she would have heard of his reputation by now. He frowns and nods. "Born again, tongue-speaking brother, huh?"

Rachel laughs. "I don't know about tongue-speaking, because people are faking that one too. But definitely a man who fears God."

"I know… 'Cause, I listen to your show. You're doing the right thing. Don't settle for less," Doug says, his eyes meeting hers.

"Thanks, Doug."

"Hmmm…" Ejike mutters.

At this point, Ekene arrives at the dining table with Rochelle on his arm. The trio turn to look at them. Rochelle's unkempt hair is a tell-tale of the mischief they'd been up to in one of the rooms in the mansion. Rachel looks around to see that almost everyone has gone, and it is already evening. Where has the time gone?

"So, you coming out with us tonight, Rache?" Ekene asks.

"No, thanks. I've got to study."

"That's a shame," Rochelle says, her tone lacking in

sincerity. "Ejike, I have a babe for you," she adds and winks at him.

Ejike looks embarrassed. He throws a quick glance at Rachel, before eyeballing Rochelle. "No, thanks. I'm good."

"No, really. Donna is really nice. She's just gotten out a relationship, and I know she's ready to have some fun! Come on!!!"

"Leave Ejike alone... He knows how to get his own women," Ekene says, forcing back his laughter.

"You guys are wicked!" Ejike says in annoyance, rising from the table to leave the room. Ekene and Rochelle follow after him with laughter.

"So, what are you really doing tonight?" Doug asks, when they are alone.

"Studying. I'm doing an online course."

"Oh, okay... I would have loved to get to know you better..."

Rachel smiles shyly, wondering how to respond to his expressed interest. "I guess another time."

"Yeah... Definitely!" he beams.

CHAPTER THREE

"Good morning, beautiful people. What are you doing this lovely, Sunday morning? Whether you're at Church, on your way to Church or sitting in front of the TV at home, holla at your girl. I'm with you all morning till the lunch hour show. Call in, and tell us what God has done for you lately…"

The lines light up and Rachel picks the first caller. "Caller on line 1…"

"Hi, Rachel. Good morning. I'm Jennifer."

"Good morning, Jennifer. Where are you calling from?"

"Ikorodu."

"Cool! So, what has He done for you lately?"

"God has been so good to me, Rachel. I just want to praise Him for getting my husband a new job! He's been out of work for almost a year, and it has been such a strain on us, with three kids and all. But he finally got a job in the industry of his choice! Glory be to God!"

"All glory! That's awesome! God is faithful! Thanks for sharing your testimony," Rachel says, as she ends the connection. "Enjoy this jam by Mary Mary, Jennifer."

Mary Mary's "Shackles" song blares loudly on the radio, as Rachel takes a music interlude. She selects two more praise jams to follow, "Victory" by Yolanda Adams and Kirk Franklin's "Stomp".

"So, how was yesterday?" Dongjap asks, when Rachel takes her headset off.

Rachel shrugs. "It was okay."

"When am I getting my invitation for the wedding?"

Rachel chuckles. "As if! We just did introduction, nau... Wedding is not for another three months."

"Sha, don't forget my IV."

"No problem."

Dongjap fidgets, wondering how to say what he wants to say. "Well, ummm… I was thinking… If you're not seeing anyone by then, maybe we can go together…?"

Rachel looks up from her computer screen, where she'd been scrolling through Facebook. Had Dongjap just asked her out? He couldn't be serious. She begins to giggle, but his expression is unmistakable. He isn't joking.

She swallows. "That's nice. But I wouldn't want to give anyone the wrong impression." *Especially you. Though it might get everybody off my back about getting married.*

"Oh, okay," Dongjap says, with a slight shrug. He'd tried, at least.

Rachel puts her headset back on, feeling a need to do something to break the awkwardness that has suddenly enveloped them. Even though the third song is still half way through, she begins to talk over it to her listeners.

Dongjap gets the message loud and clear. They will never be more than friends.

***

Rachel couldn't stop thinking about Dongjap's proposal at the studio today. Had she really done the right thing to have brushed him off, just like that? Would it really have been so bad to have him as her date on such an important occasion, when she would be otherwise bombarded with questions about her love life?

But what if she doesn't meet anyone for years? Would she have to keep a stand-in guy to keep up appearances of a blossoming relationship? How far was she willing to go to deceive others? And wouldn't she just end up deceiving herself, or worse, find herself married to the place-holder boyfriend? She shudders to think of such an eventuality.

No, she had done the right thing. It was an act of faith and sincerity to tell him the truth and not give him false hope. Now, if only she knew what to do about Mr Right's absence. She missed him so much…

Suddenly, her mobile phone beeps with a notification. Rachel checks and finds a friendship request from one Douglas Olumide. She frowns, as she doesn't know anyone by that name. When she clicks to see who their five mutual friends are, she realises that he is in fact the Doug she met yesterday evening, and she decides to accept his request.

Immediately, a message comes through from him on Messenger. *"Hi, beautiful! How are you?"*

Rachel lets out a sigh. She doesn't feel much like chatting, but she doesn't want to be rude. *"Hi, Doug. I'm good. You?"*

"Great! Listened to your show this morning. I was blessed."

Rachel beams instantly, finding his affirmation endearing. He seems to be genuinely interested in her. *But is he also genuine about God*, she wonders?

"Thanks!"

"You're welcome. So, when do you get to go to Church?" *I guess that answers it*, she thinks.

"I'm on rotation with another radio host, so I'm only on once a fortnight. I usually make evening service, though, whenever I'm on air in the morning."

"Awesome! Cos, I wouldn't want you to miss out on the Word now…"

Hmmm… Rachel thinks to herself. He seems a bit patronising, or is he just genuinely concerned about her spiritual development? She decides that she'd let the statement fly.

In the silence that follows, she gets notifications of his likes and comments on her recent pictures and posts. She becomes alarmed when he starts liking all her older pictures and posts too. *Stalker alert!*

Be cool. He's clearly into you, she thinks to calm her nerves. She decides to return the favour by checking out his posts and pictures too.

He doesn't have as many. He's in mostly group pictures, usually taken at parties and weddings. By the look of things, there isn't a woman in his life. And aside from pictures, his timeline is littered with memes and jokes about a host of different things. She likes a few of them and then gets tired of the activity.

Unfortunately, her modest activity on his page seems to spur him on to keep liking and commenting on her photos, and even share a couple with her in their chat, asking her questions about where and when they were taken. To cut short their interaction, she sends him a 'brb' message and closes the Messenger app on her phone. *Jeez, he's intense,* she thinks.

***

The rains are early this year. Fat drops of water fall and make small puddles on the recently manicured lawn in the Eden mansion, and the wind makes a whistling sound through the short pine trees that line the garden. The air is moist and thick, carrying with it the fragrance of the flowers mixed with the stench of manure and stank water from the overflowing gutters on the street.

Rachel watches as their staff below run through the rain to attend to various tasks. The servant girl is hastily packing the sheets she'd just washed this morning. *Poor girl,* Rachel thinks. *She's going to have to wash them again.*

Sitting back, safely sheltered in the second-floor balcony of her family home, Rachel turns the page in the book she's reading. It's a book about Christian dating and marriage, one of many books she has been reading to grow her knowledge and understanding about faith-based marriage. Her counselling course, though rich in information about ethical practices and psychological insights, lacks the Christian perspective she desires to also gain.

Through the sound of the rain, Rachel hears her phone ringing inside. She goes to check the mobile where she left it charging. It's fully charged, and she unplugs it. An unidentified person is calling her. She slides her finger across the screen to accept the call.

"Hello?"

"The voice of an angel!"

"Hello? Who's this please?" Rachel strains to hear the caller. The network connection isn't good, but she thinks she heard a man say, "the voice of an angel". *How creepy...* She isn't sure she's interested in the call, but she at least wants to confirm who is calling and why.

"Hey, Rachel. It's Doug. How are you doing?"

Rachel's surprised and a little irritated, but she's not sure why. *How did he get my number?* But that is a silly question. Who else would have given him, if not Rochelle?

"I'm fine, Doug. What's up?"

"I'm in Ikoyi, and I thought of you. What you up to today?"

"A few things. Kinda busy."

"This rain has got me stranded here. I was about to hit the Third Mainland bridge when it started pouring. Can I come wait it out at yours?"

"Ummm... How do you know I'm home?"

"I just figured you would be. You're not on air this afternoon. I told you I'm a listener. I actually wanted to call into your show today."

Is he for real?! "Yeah, Wednesday's my day off."

"Cool. So, can I stop by? I'll leave as soon as the rain lets up. *Please...*"

"I guess..."

"Yeah! You'll see me now..."

Moments later, Rachel sees a car pull in front of her house and the horn go off. *Really?!*

***

Rachel goes down to open the door for Doug. He's looking taller and more handsome than she remembered. Well, she hadn't really taken much notice of him before. When she looked back on the day they met, the sun only shined on Ejike's face. She knew she was attracted to him. Thank goodness he wasn't the one pestering her right now. *God would surely not give us more than we can bear,* she thinks, as an amused smile plays on her lips.

Doug laughs. "I know, I must look a mess. This rain is unmerciful!"

She looks at him as he shakes rainwater from his thick arms. His shirt is clinging to his well-built frame. *Hmmm... Not a bad looker at all.* She swallows. She thinks that he actually looks better with the rugged look he has going on than the clean-shaven, school-boy look he had last Saturday.

"You're a bit of a shorty, aren't you?" he says, causing her to look down at the bathroom slippers she is wearing.

On Saturday, she'd chosen to wear a pair of four-inch heels, as the sandals went well with the ankara dress and made her slim legs look longer. Now, she had on some old denim shorts and a pink, cotton t-shirt. She loved to dress for comfort and hadn't thought to change before opening the door.

Rachel gave a small smile in response and moved aside for Doug to enter her home. Again, she wondered why she hadn't just said "no". What was he really doing at her house? Still, her good manners prevailed.

"Do you want something to drink?" she asks.

He beams at her. "Please! Nothing cold though...

Thanks."

Rachel leads him into the guest living room downstairs, before leaving him and heading for the kitchen.

***

An hour later, the heavy rain has turned to some light drizzling, and the May sun shines brightly through the clouds. The atmosphere smells cleansed, though the waters have left the road flooded in parts. Rachel looks over at her companion who has been on his phone for the last half an hour, sending messages on social media. He must be very popular, she thinks.

"The rain has stopped," she says, hesitantly.

He looks up and smiles at her. "You want me to leave?"

Rachel shrugs. "I was just saying…"

"It's okay. I get it. I need to get going too," he says, putting his phone away. "But I really enjoyed spending time with you like this. Even if we didn't say much."

"I'm sorry. This is the only time I get to read. But it was nice to have you over too," she admits.

He beams. "Really?" She smiles. "So, we can do it again… Like, I can take you out on a proper date and get to know you?"

Rachel lets out a sigh. "Well… Actually… I'm not dating at the moment."

"Why?"

"I just want to be led… And I also don't really have the time."

"Hmmm… Well, I'm not going anywhere! I have all the time, and I want you. So, I'll wait, until you're ready."

She swallows. Wow, so straight forward. Maybe he was worth considering. She'd have to pray about it. "Okay."

She escorts him downstairs to the front door, and he pulls her in for a hug before making his exit. As he heads to his car, Rochelle and Ekene drive in. Rachel lingers at the door, as Doug waits to greet the couple before getting in his car and driving off.

"Wow, you don't waste time!" Rochelle teases, when she and Ekene get to the front door.

"It's not what it looks like."

"I bet!" Rochelle laughs, but Ekene doesn't look amused. He looks into Rachel's eyes, searching for something, but she quickly looks away from him. He decides not to say anything. If she actually likes Doug, then it's none of his business.

Rachel doesn't know what to make of the look she just received from Ekene. Was that concern or jealousy? It was strange how it felt like disappointment, like he thought that she wasn't the good girl she presented herself to be. But who was he to judge her? She hadn't done anything wrong…and besides, it's none of his business.

CHAPTER FOUR

It's the day of Rochelle's traditional wedding, and the house is in an uproar. In every room, there are aunties at work making preparations and last-minute adjustments to things. Aunty Faith is busy making adjustments to Mrs Eden's blouse in her bedroom; Aunty Blessing is tying the gele for the bridesmaids in the family living room; Aunty Joy is doing the bride's make-up in her bedroom; Aunty Patricia is supervising the caterers in the kitchen, while Aunty Eloho is supervising those setting up canopies and chairs outside.

In the spa room, Mrs Eden is getting herself pampered. Two aunties are with her, making sure that her pedicure, manicure and facial are exceptional. And the wedding planner is overseeing all that is going on, coordinating with the band, the performers and other vendors to ensure that the occasion is a wonderful success.

Rachel doesn't have any work assigned to her. She also needs to get herself made-up, styled and dressed, and be there to assist her sister with anything she needs. Their cousins are also on ground for quick errands. The only people who seem to be idle are the privileged sons and older, married fathers, who are already dressed and chatting in the guest lounge downstairs, where the TV is blaring in competition with the

DJ outside.

"Looking good!" Aunty Blessing says to Rachel, when she'd done with her gele. "Today is the day you will meet your own husband! Don't worry about a thing," she adds and winks at her.

Rachel manages a smile. *It's going to be a long day!* Rising up, she leaves to check on her sister.

"Isn't she gorgeous?!" Aunty Joy beams at Rochelle. "Such a beautiful face."

"Thank you, aunty!" Rochelle says, admiring her reflection in the mirror. She notices Rachel at the door. "You look nice… But your gele looks too tight."

"It's okay," Rachel mutters, using her finger to adjust it on her ear.

"Come and sit down, let me touch you up…" Aunty Joy beckons to Rachel, when Rochelle stands up to go to the bathroom.

"I'm okay, Aunty…"

"Abeg, come siddun!" Aunty Joy hisses. "You don't know that after Rochelle, all eyes are on you? Isn't it bad enough that she should marry before you, and then you don't even want to look your best?!"

Rachel sits down to avoid more talk on the subject, but it doesn't stop Aunty Joy.

"When I was your age, I already had two children, oh," she continues.

***

"Hey…"

Rachel looks up to see who owned the deep, sultry voice. She is face to face with Ejike. How hadn't she seen him coming?

"Hey," she smiles back.

"What a party! Are you enjoying yourself?"

She shrugs. "Yeah, thanks. Are you?"

"Honestly?" he asks, cheekily.

She looks into his eyes. They are deep and seem to swallow her in. "Hmmm hmm…"

He leans in and whispers. "I am now…"

She can't help the beam that breaks open her lips into a wide smile, and then a giggle. "You're funny!"

Ejike also giggles. "I'm glad you think so… If that's a good thing."

She shrugs. "Hmmm…"

"You don't talk much," he observes.

Rachel takes in a deep breath. It was a good observation. "I reserve my energy for the radio station. I'm not very social in real life, unfortunately."

"I get. You look good, though…"

She instinctively looks down at her two-piece native attire, which she'd thought was unflattering. She didn't really like the colour, and it was a bit itchy in places, but it sure made her boobs look big, she'd noticed. She decides to be polite and accept the compliment. Looking into his face, she smiles and says, "Thanks."

"Hey, beautiful!"

The enchantment is broken, and Rachel tears her face away to look at Doug, who just joined them. She'd almost forgotten that they were in a party, in a big open room filled with all her family. Her heart rate increases suddenly, as she takes in all the noise and commotion of the wedding.

"Hi, Doug," she mutters breathily. He pulls her in for a hug, and then slaps palms with Ejike, whose demeanour has changed.

"What's up?" Doug asks, looking between the pair, his arm still holding Rachel close, though she seems uncomfortable. She eventually releases herself from his embrace, and leans back against the wall.

"Nothing… Just chatting," Ejike says. He looks between Rachel and Doug. Sensing that there's something between them, he makes an excuse to leave. He swallows. "Let me go see how Ekene's doing. Talk to you later."

"Yeah, mehn!" Doug says, smiling gratefully at his friend.

Rachel watches after Ejike, wondering when they'd have a chance to chat again. For some reason, she liked him. He made her heart smile, which was a very rare occurrence. What was it about him?

"A penny for your thoughts…"

Rachel looks up at Doug. She'd almost forgotten that he was still there. She swallows. "I just remembered that I need to do something…" she says, stepping away.

"Oh, okay. We can catch up later."

"Yeah…" *Oh my God… I just lied to that man!*

***

"Do you take this man…?"

The minister is taking the young couple through their vows, in the presence of their family and friends. Rachel ponders on the vows and the significance of each promise, as her sister says "I do" to each one. She wonders at the maturity of the pair who are making these declarations. Do they not have doubts? Closing her eyes, she prays for their marriage, that God would make them able to abide and honour their vows as long as they live.

The church is beautifully decorated with ribbons and flowers, plus the colourful aso'ebi of the wedding party and guests adds radiance to the hall. The bride looks exquisite in white; the best Rachel has ever seen her look. And her full, dark brown locks are pinned up on her head in a gorgeous style fit for the front page of Black Hair magazine. The groom is looking tall and handsome, and he seems to have eyes only for his bride, who is beaming from ear to ear.

"I now pronounce you husband and wife! You may kiss your bride," the minister says.

The room comes alive with applause as Ekene takes Rochelle in his arms to kiss her sweetly in the presence of all. Afterwards, they both turn to face the congregation and raise their hands in unity and triumph. They are married!

Rachel smiles. She is startled by a tap on her shoulder. It's Aunty Faith. She looks nervously at her aunty, hoping and praying she won't make any remark about her own love life or lack of.

"Next year, it will be you up there!" But if only pigs could fly…

***

The bridesmaids are all wearing a satin, baby pink fabric they styled themselves. One of them looks like she wasn't informed what occasion she was sewing for. Her mini-dress is scandalous to say the least. Rachel grimaces as she turns her face away from the breasts spilling out of the dress.

She looks down at her own modest gown. Apart from the waist, where it hugs her body, the fuchsia pink dress flows out into a bell shape, stopping just below her knees, leaving her slender calves on display. On her feet are silver, low-heeled sandals, because she was anticipating being on her feet for many hours today.

"*Sexy Cinderella!*" someone sings.

Rachel is now familiar with the sound of Doug's drawl. For some reason, he seems to have taken the impression that they are dating or something. Since the day he came over to her home uninvited, he hasn't stopped taking liberties to encroach on her life and space. He'd stopped by the studio on multiple occasions, using one excuse or the other about why he was in the neighbourhood. He even met with her producer and said he too is a producer. She'd done a double take that day!

"*Yes, I get music artists signed up,*" he'd explained, before bringing out a CD for Dongjap to preview. "*Check that out! It's a jam!*"

She'd humoured him once, and allowed him to take her out to lunch. They'd eaten meat pie and scotch egg at the Tantalizers near her office. He'd talked about how beautiful she looked, even without make-up.

"*You're just so natural and real! You're really special, Rachel…*" he'd said.

"*Thanks,*" she'd muttered in response.

She looks up into his happy face. He always seems so happy, like he's got a secret or something. "Hey, Doug."

"You look…" he pauses for dramatic effect, "amazing!"

Rachel lets out a deep breath. "Thanks! You look good too."

"Thanks, Rachel."

Without warning, he takes hold of her hand and pulls her unto the dance floor, where he proceeds to dance with her. Rochelle and Ekene are lost in each other, dancing and being cheered on by friends. Rachel notices Ejike among the groomsmen, and he looks away when their eyes meet. She feels a little disappointed, hoping he would have looked at her long enough to communicate "hi".

But who cares…? It's fine. She looks at her dance partner and decides to let the music take control.

"Wow! So, you can dance like this?!" Doug exclaims, holding on to Rachel as she wiggles her body to the music, turning some attention from the bride.

When Rochelle notices that she's no longer the centre of attention, she goes to join her sister, and begins to twerk on the dance floor. There is an uproar among the guys as they compare the sisters. Rochelle's moves are so scandalous that her husband has to go and remind everyone that "this one is married"! He pulls her into his arms, laughing as he pats her big butt affectionately.

"You go wound person, oh," he jokes in her ear, and she giggles.

"Mehn… You are full of surprises, Rachel! Chai! I think I love you…" Doug blurts out and brings Rachel back to her senses.

She looks about, wondering about the damage of her

actions; letting go and dancing provocatively, like she used to. There are a lot of guys looking at her differently. Some have grins on their faces, like they knew she was a vixen all along, and others wink to indicate their interest. She, however, is more concerned about the blank stare she gets from Ejike. He doesn't look impressed.

"I have to sit down. I'm tired," she says to Doug, hastening to get as far from the dance floor as possible.

***

"What are you doing here all by yourself?"

Rachel looks up to find her Aunty Patricia looking down at her. The older woman pulls a chair out and takes a seat. Rachel puts her phone away and smiles at her aunty.

"I'm just taking a break, Aunty."

"Oh, my dear… Are you sad that it's not your wedding?" she asks, presumptuously. "Don't worry, dear, your own will come! But you will not meet anybody sitting here by yourself."

Rachel leans her head on her hand, with her elbow on the table, rubbing her forehead to massage away a growing pain. Why couldn't her aunties just give her a break already? *But I guess they just want me to be happy*, she thinks. "No, aunty. I'm not sad…"

"You could have fooled me, dear… Do you even have a boyfriend?"

Jeez! "I'm taking a break from dating…"

"For *what*?!" Aunty Patricia exclaims. "Are you one of those Feminists?! Please oh, don't do that to your parents, Rachel…"

"Aunty…"

"Hey, there you are!"

It's the first time Rachel has been pleased to hear Doug's voice interrupt a conversation. She turns to him, smiling with sweet relief. "Hey!"

"Been looking for you since…" Doug continues, then

turns to look at Rachel's aunty. "Good evening, ma."

"Good evening, my son." She looks at Rachel for an introduction. When Rachel doesn't make one, she decides to ask. "Are you Rachel's boyfriend?"

Rachel is mortified and looks at Doug with a pleading look on her face.

He beams. "Yes, ma… Rachel is the love of my life. I can't wait for the day she'll be my wife."

Rachel shuts her eyes against that image and opens them to find her aunty beaming at her. "Oh, wow, Rachel! Your boyfriend is so romantic!"

Rachel swallows and says nothing. Doug settles into the seat next to her and holds her hand affectionately on the table. "Nice to meet you, aunty!"

Aunty Patricia takes that as her cue. She rises from her seat, and makes the most inappropriate demand; "When you're ready to propose, make sure you see *me* first."

Doug laughs. "Yes, ma'am!"

Rachel releases her hand from Doug's when her aunty has gone out of sight. "Thanks," is all she can mutter.

"No need to thank me, babe. I meant every word. I just want to be the one who makes you happy…"

Rachel swallows and looks at Doug.

"Am I asking for too much?"

She shakes her head and he smiles.

CHAPTER FIVE

"So, ummm… Something going on between you and Rachel…?

Doug smiles smugly at his long-time friend and former neighbour. They are still at the wedding, and he'd just left Rachel to get a bottle of champagne at the bar. She said she didn't want to dance nor mingle, and just wanted to sit and observe for a while. She was clearly the quiet type, but that was cool with him. He was just glad that she was happy chilling with him.

"Yeah… We're taking it slow but, mehn, I got it bad…"

"Hmmm," Ejike swallows. "I thought she was one of those "set-apart born-againers", though…"

"What? And I'm not?!" Doug pulls a frown, and when Ejike just stares back at him, he breaks into a laugh. "Look, mehn, that's old me. In Christ, all things are new… And for her, I'm ready to be anything she wants…"

Ejike swallows and nods, as he figures out what's really going on. "You can't lie to her, Doug. You can't hurt her…"

Doug looks at his friend, whose gaze is a little weaker than normal. He realises that Ejike also has a thing for Rachel. Well, too bad… He got her first. "You don't have to worry about her, mehn... This one is serious. I'm playing for keeps!"

Ejike smiles slightly at Doug's wink. He wants to believe that Doug has nothing but good intentions for Rachel, but he is still very doubtful. But what can he really do?

Now that Doug has made it clear that he is serious about Rachel, he would have to step aside and give them room, just as he would expect Doug to, if he'd been the one to get to her first. He looks over at where Rachel's sitting and feels his heart twist. *Damn!* Why had he listened to Ekene and not gone after what he wanted? If Doug could get her...well, maybe she wasn't that special...

No, she is. He is sure of it. He just missed his chance.

***

The sun's high in the sky today. Rachel wonders if that's why they call it "Sunday", as this one day of the week is usually characterised with sunshine and bright clouds in Nigeria. She takes in a deep sigh as she looks out of the window of one of the jeeps, on a convoy to take Rochelle to her husband's family house, as is the tradition.

She suddenly thinks of seeing Ejike again. They hadn't spoken much at the reception yesterday. After she'd embarrassed herself on the dance floor, she couldn't bear to look in his eyes again. *Why do I care so much about what he thinks*, she ponders?

But she already knew why. She had a crush. She'd had those before. Usually for men that were not good for her, as she was sure he wasn't. *"Be careful, sha. He has a reputation..."* she very clearly remembers Rochelle saying.

Taking in a deep breath, she renews her resolve. She won't let this crush turn into anything more. She would have to do her best to keep him at arm's length today and out of her mind permanently.

As they drive into the Okafor's expansive land, off the Lagos/Ibadan expressway, she hears Richard marvel,

"Wow… They're loaded!" Knowing how well-off their father is, that was certainly saying something.

Her eyes roam the grounds, which appear to belong to a holiday resort. So many tropical trees, exotic flowers, perfectly maintained lawns and tastefully constructed buildings take up the space, leaving a pathway to the main mansion. There is even a medium-sized artificial lake, which they drive over on a stone bridge to get to the driveway and car park of the mansion. "Wow," she can't but marvel. *Rochelle hit the jackpot!*

***

"In Jesus' name! In the mighty name of Jesus!"

Mrs Eden is leading the prayers for her daughter and her new husband, as she leaves her with his family. It's an emotional time for all involved, and Rochelle is in tears. Rachel's eyes are closed as she mutters "Amen," to her stepmother's prayer points.

"No weapon formed against this union shall prosper! Every evil eye that is looking at you, let them go blind in Jesus' name!" Mrs Eden continues.

"Amen!" is shouted out in unison.

Aunty Joy, who had followed them for the handover, is jumping up and down. Rachel can feel her movements beside her, and she opens her eyes briefly when her aunty knocks her by accident. When she looks across the room, she catches Ejike eyes, and he quickly shuts them. A smile grows on her face as she closes her eyes again and says "Amen!"

"Lord, You are the one that has brought Your children together. Keep them together by Your mighty hand! No wicked intruder shall tear them asunder! We rebuke divorce in Jesus' name!"

"Amen!"

The prayers continue, as Aunty Eloho picks off where Mrs Eden stops. It is another twenty minutes before they finally round off. Rachel is glad when Aunty Joy ends her prayer with "...in Jesus mighty name we have prayed!"

***

"What time is your flight tomorrow?" Rachel asks Rochelle, after they share a hug.

"We're leaving in the evening."

"Okay, cool! I'm so happy for you, sis!"

"Thanks, Rache," Rochelle says sincerely.

"Take good care of my sister, will you?" Rachel says to Ekene, as they hug.

"No doubt," he replies, with a grin.

"Alright... I'll see you guys later..."

"I don't get a goodbye?" Ejike says, unable to resist the urge to get Rachel's attention.

She beams at him and moves to hug him too. His torso is firmer than she imagined. He's obviously a man committed to a work-out regime. He pulls her in, and her body seems to fit into his, like ying and yang. She closes her eyes, smelling him. Musky and masculine. She swallows and withdraws.

He's looking at her with longing. He didn't want to let her go... Her brief presence in his arms had him unbalanced, but yet so exhilarated. From the look on her face, she'd felt it too. She belonged in his arms.

"Let me walk you to the car..." he doesn't know when the words come out, but he's happy when she nods and waves at her sister. Thank goodness Doug hadn't come. Today was strictly family and, thankfully, the Okafors' home is a far distance from the inner city, so not that convenient for him to make an appearance.

As they walk, he's stuck for what to say. "It's a shame we never got to meet before," he finally utters.

Rachel sports a small smile, as she turns sideways to glance at Ejike. "Yeah, I guess."

They stop at her car. Her parents are still saying their goodbyes. "I see you and Doug are getting rather close..."

Rachel swallows, unsure how to answer that. She rather shrugs. "He's cool."

"Yes, he is…" Ejike mutters.

Rachel notices his demeanour changing. She's not quite ready to say goodbye. "So, you live in Port Harcourt?"

Ejike nods. "Yeah… For now."

"When are you going back?"

"Tomorrow."

"Oh, okay." *I guess that's for the best*, she thinks. "Well, travel safe!"

"Yeah, thanks," he says, backing away as she opens the door to enter her vehicle. "Take it easy, Rache."

She doesn't know what to say, so she simply smiles and gets into the car. He waves goodbye as he steps aside. The engine sounds, and the jeep begins to pull away. Rachel forces her eyes to leave Ejike's back. She swallows. *It's better this way…*

But she can't help the sadness that lingers, though the day remains bright and sunny. *Lord, please watch over my heart… I only want Your best for me*, she prays in her spirit.

***

Ryan and Richard settle on the sofa to watch a football match as soon as they get home. Rachel decides to join them, but the game proves too boring, with no one scoring within the first 30 minutes. There had only been a couple of near misses too. Quietly, she rises up to go to her room.

On her bed, she browses her social media applications, thinking to catch up with her friends. But apart from a few likes and comments on the pictures she'd posted yesterday of her sister's wedding, there were no messages to respond to. She decides to reach out to a few of them.

"*Hey, Rache! Sorry I couldn't come yesterday. I saw the pictures tho! Congrats to Rochelle* 😎" is Anita's response.

"*Hi, Rachel! How are you?*" Omilola replies.

"*I'm good. How are you?*"

"I'm great, dear. Sorry I had to leave early yesterday! But I saw you getting down with that Doug! Hmmm…"

"Lol! I was just being silly."

"I didn't even know you guys knew each other."

"We don't really… I just met him a couple of months ago. Why? You know him?"

"Well, not him per se. I know his ex. Anyway, sha… I guess people can change, but just be careful."

"I will. I'm not even into him, so…"

"Well, that's good. Look, let me holla at you later…"

"Sure. Thanks for coming!"

"It was my pleasure."

Rachel sighs after closing their chat. So, a lot of people had seen her getting down with Doug on the dance floor. She should have been more careful about the impression she was sending. *Oh, well…*

There's a knock on her door. "Come in!"

"Hey, Rache," Richard says. "There's someone here to see you…"

"Oh, really? I'm coming."

"Aight…"

***

Rachel checks her reflection in the mirror and slips into something more comfortable. Checking the time on her phone, she confirms that it's just after 5 pm, and still early evening. Who could be visiting now?

He is sitting on the arm of the sofa, facing the widescreen TV. The football match is now in overtime, and the men are riveted to the screen. He turns to look at her as she descends the stairs. He stands up, smiling, and approaches her.

"Hey, beautiful!"

Rachel takes in a deep breath. "Hey, Doug. What's up?"

She alights the last step, and he swoops her into his arms for an embrace. She's happy when he releases her. She notices Ryan turn their way briefly, before returning his attention to the game that's on.

"I thought you could do with some company. I mean, now that Rochelle's gone…"

"I'm fine, actually."

"Yeah, I know," he makes a lame joke. She doesn't smile. "What can I say? I wanted to see you… How are you?"

"Fine…"

"Goal!!!" Richard shouts, leaping from his seat! Their eyes turn to the TV screen, as footballers race across the field, high-fiving and jumping on each other.

"Good game!" Ryan mutters coolly.

"Wow! That was quite a shot," Doug says, as the replay is shown on the screen.

Rachel just looks on at the men. Doug returns his attention to his friend. "I guess you're not into football…"

"Not much…"

"Let's go for a walk…"

Rachel hesitates. "Ummm…"

"Please… I'm not going to bite… You're safe, trust me."

She lets out a breath. "Okay."

***

"So, how was it today?" Doug asks as they walk along the estate. He wants to hold her hand, but she's holding them behind her back.

"It was good."

"I couldn't come, because I had stuff to do at church," he says, as explanation for his absence.

"Oh, okay," she mutters. He seems to be rather active in church. He'd even invited her to an event at his church once, but the notice had been too short, and she had other things to do that day.

"There's a programme happening next Sunday. I'm actually one of the organisers. It's a bit of a concert. Can you come?"

"What time?"

"About 5pm?"

"Hmmm… It sounds good!"

"Great! Then it's a date!"

Rachel stops and turns to him. He's looking at her sweetly. She swallows. "Ummm… Doug, it's not. A date, I mean. We're just friends, okay?"

He shrugs. "Yeah, I know… I was just saying…"

"I just don't want to lead you on or anything. I'm not in that place. Can we just keep this friendly?"

"Sure."

She smiles and continues walking. "Thanks!"

CHAPTER SIX

The auditorium is packed full. The music is blaring through the large speakers, and the lyrics have deep meaning. Rachel is immersed in the concert experience as a local Christian band leads the crowd in praise and worship.

"*You are the reason I am living...*" the congregation sings along with the band, hands in the air and eyes closed in awe. Rachel sings aloud, allowing herself to ride on the euphoria to a higher sense of God's presence and majesty. She meditates on the lyrics, allowing the tears to flow as she feels the weight of the emotions.

"You are the reason, Lord," she says as she is ushered into prayer by the Holy Spirit. "Who is like unto You, Father?! Lord, I never want to be found without You. Without You, I am lost..."

An applause rings through the hall at the completion of the worship song. Rachel continues in prayer, her heart heavy with all the things she wants to say to God. She hears a female preacher take the microphone and talk about how wonderful the worship experience has been tonight. She tells them that one more musician will be taking the stage and invites the audience to welcome him generously with their applause.

Rachel concludes her prayer and joins in the applause. She looks about, feeling fortunate that she'd been able to get a seat with a good view. Doug had actually reserved space for her, and she had been surprised to discover that he was a hit at the church. He really had been influential in getting this programme organised, and she couldn't help but feel some pride at knowing him.

"That's my guy right there! He's going to be the next big thing in gospel," Doug shouts at Rachel, through the fanatic chaos as the heralded musician takes the stage.

Right away, the atmosphere changes to rock, and the message is about making it, deliverance from struggles and the glory of the believers that is received by grace alone. The crowd seems to love his modern style, which incorporates rap with rhythm and blues. Rachel is both entertained and inspired.

"He's really good!" she shouts at Doug.

He beams at her. "I'm glad you're loving it! Thanks for coming!"

"Yeah, thanks for the invite!" she smiles back.

They both turn back towards the stage and dance and sing along to the musician's jam!

***

"Hi, Rachel, I'm Leona from Ikota."

"Hi, Leona! Good to have you on the show. What would you like to **Ask Rachel**?" Rachel smiles, loving how she is able to incorporate the title of her new show into her pitch. With her counselling qualification gained last month, she now feels qualified to give relationship advice to her listeners.

"It's been six months since my husband and I had sex, and I'm getting worried that he's getting his pleasure outside. What should I do?"

"Hmmm... Wow, six months is a long time! Can I know what you've done or tried to do to change the situation?"

"Well, I've tried not to nag him. I've tried to entice him

with my dressing and cooking. I've even tried to schedule time together. But he will just cancel or not even bother to come home. When I try to seduce him, he complains that he's busy or tired. I don't understand why he keeps rejecting me!"

"I'm so sorry about your experience, Leona. Please try not to jump to conclusions. Would you say that your husband is a trustworthy and honest person?"

"Yes… He's very passionate about God. He likes to do the right thing."

"That's great! Your trust in him is important right now. As long as he has shown himself to be trustworthy, continue to give him your trust. It may also help to put yourself in his shoes. What sorts of burdens is he dealing with right now? Has there been a recent crisis; at home or with his business or even health? Even if nothing obvious comes to mind, there could be emotional, social or developmental challenges his grappling with, and he may be feeling overwhelmed."

"We have been having some financial challenges, but…"

"I mean, everyone has these challenges, and they are not really an excuse for his behaviour, but just a way for you to understand him, and make room for him. I really think you should seek an opportunity to talk to your husband about what you've observed and how you've been feeling. You can remind him that you still respect him and find him sexually attractive. He may not actually feel respected or attractive to you."

"Okay… I have tried to talk about it, though…"

"I understand. Don't stop trying. If you really think you can't get him to hear you, then it's time you invite a mediator to help you guys communicate again, and work on the other issues in your marriage."

"Thanks, Rachel. So, you don't think he's cheating?"

"I don't think it will help you to go down that route now. Give him that benefit of the doubt and work with trust, until proven otherwise. No one likes to be made a fool of, but if you accuse him or treat him as a cheater without proof, you might just make a fool of yourself. So, let's think positively first and build on love."

"Thanks so much! I'll try to talk to him again. God bless you, Rachel!"

"God bless you too."

***

"*Great show today!*"

Rachel smiles upon receiving the message on WhatsApp from Doug. He is turning out to be her biggest fan. Even though he stopped visiting the studio and reduced his visits to her home, he still contacts her on a daily basis, sending her encouraging messages, Bible passages and invites to special events he learns about.

"*Thanks, Doug! How's your day going?*"

"*It's been good, thanks. Normal hustle.*"

"*Lol! One day, one day, it's will all connect!*" Rachel types back, borrowing lyrics from Naden's jam, "One Day, One Day". It has become one of her favourite jams, since she heard him perform at the concert. She even plays his song on the radio during her Sunday praise sessions.

"😂😁 *When you know, you know!*" Doug sends back.

"*Aight… Later :)*"

Rachel looks over their chat and can't help smiling, thinking about how far they've come. She's now able to call Doug a friend and mean it. Though she's aware that he still likes her differently, they've both been able to steer away from any dating talk. And she finds his respect for her decision and continued friendship to be endearing. Most men would have just walked away, knowing that nothing was ever going to happen.

She lets out a sigh. Thoughts of Ejike play on her mind. She wonders what he might be doing that very second. *Does he ever think of me*, she wonders? *Why has he never bothered to get in touch?* Again, she wonders, *why should I care?*

***

"Hi guys! My birthday's coming up next Saturday, and I'd like to visit an orphanage and take some provisions for the children. They also have a library that needs new computers! Would you be interested in coming along? And could you help to raise funds? Regards, Rachel."

Doug smiles upon seeing the broadcast message from Rachel. So, her birthday's coming up. And this is how she wants to celebrate? *I could get down with that…*

"This is a great initiative, Rache. Count me in!" he types back.

"Thanks, Doug!"

He knows a few people who would be happy to donate to a cause such as this. He decides to make calls to solicit for their support.

"Hey, Ejike! Been a while…"

***

Ejike is surprised to hear from Doug. They haven't spoken since he returned to Port Harcourt weeks ago. They actually aren't as close as when they were kids, but Doug is hard to shake. When he's determined to be your friend, he sticks to you like glue.

"Hey… What's up?" he replies.

"Not much, mehn! How's PH?"

"Same ol', same ol'."

"Okay… I've got this thing I'm organising with a friend. She wants to celebrate her birthday by visiting an orphanage and giving them new computers too. I promised I'd help raise funds… Can you help?"

"Who's this friend?"

Doug is hesitant to say, but realises that Ejike might soon find out anyway. "It's Rachel."

"Oh… When's her birthday?"

"It's next Saturday. So, can you help?"

"Ummm… Yeah, I can send something. Let her send me the details on my WhatsApp."

"I can just forward it to you, though. I'm sort of handling it."

"I understand. I'd still like to express my wishes, so give her my number, will you?"

"Sure. Thanks, Ejike."

"No problem, man. Later!"

***

"*Hi guys! Plans have been confirmed for tomorrow. Thanks so much for all the support you've shown. We've raised more than enough donations, and we will be donating half a dozen desktop computers and three laptops for the orphanage! Let's meet on location at 10 am. I'll send the Google coordinates shortly. Regards, Rachel!*"

"*Hey, Rache! I'm just seeing this. Well done! I'll make my contribution. I'm sorry, I won't be able to come,*" Ekene replies Rachel's broadcast.

"*Awww, thanks, Ekene! That's awesome. You can use the link to make your donation. God bless you, bro.*"

"*It's my pleasure!*"

Ekene clicks on the link and follows through to send his donation. He wonders if Ejike is aware of Rachel's event and decides to call him up.

"Hey, bro… How far?"

"I dey oh," Ejike replies. "What's up?"

"Do you know Rachel's having something tomorrow at an orphanage? She's raising funds for it."

"Yeah… Doug told me… I asked him to give her my number so she could send me more details, but I haven't heard from her."

"Really? Well, I'll send you her number then. You cool?"

"Yes, I am! And thanks! Have a good one!"

When their call is concluded, Ekene shares Rachel's contact with Ejike via WhatsApp.

***

Ejike looks at Rachel's contact info on his phone for a while. He had intentionally not asked for it before, because he wanted to give Doug the space to form a relationship with her, which he had expressed his desire to. But now that he has her number and is aware that she's celebrating her birthday tomorrow, he knows that he will call her. He just doesn't know what to say…

Instead of calling, he decides to send her a message on WhatsApp.

"*Hi, Rachel. This is Ejike. How are you?*"

His message is delivered, but not yet received. After a few minutes the double tick appears, but she hasn't read it yet. He decides to send another message.

"*I heard about your birthday plans! I'd like to send my support.*"

Instant double tick. Then the blue ticks appear. She has read his messages. And now, she's typing…

"*Hey, Ejike! Wow, how are you?*"

"*Am good. And you?*"

"*Awesome, thanks! I appreciate the support too, thanks. Are you in town?*"

"*No…*"

"*Okay. Well, we've already raised the funds, but we can present the charity with a cheque too. I'm sure they've got other administrative needs.*"

"*Certainly. Let me have the account details for the transfer.*"

"*Aight… I'll send them right away! Thanks so much!*"

"*No problem at all…*"

"*How did you hear about it, by the way?*"

"*Doug told me.*"

"*Oh, cool. He's been quite helpful with raising funds. I'll have to thank him.*"

"*Sure…*"

When he receives the payment info from Rachel, he makes his own contribution. It's clear to him that Doug never got back to Rachel to give her his number. He is obviously afraid of him getting in touch with Rachel. It makes him wonder just what sort of relationship Doug actually has with

Rachel... Well, it's time he stops hiding in the side-lines, especially when Doug isn't fighting fair.

"Oh, wow! I just saw your contribution! God bless you!"

Ejike beams. *"God bless you too, Rachel. You have a good heart. I'm happy to support."*

Rachel sends back three big hugs, and Ejike replies with a big grin. *Let the games begin!*

CHAPTER SEVEN

Rachel wakes up to birthday greetings on her WhatsApp. She smiles when she sees that so many of her friends remembered and chose to celebrate her with private and public messages. A few even feature her on their DP or Instagram or Facebook feeds.

She spends the first thirty minutes of her waking moments replying messages. She's not surprised to see that Doug left a greeting for her on every social media platform they are both on. On WhatsApp, he'd sent her a voice note, singing "Happy Birthday to You!"

She replies, "Awww... This is so sweet of you! Thanks :)"

He replies with the hug and kiss emojis.

She receives a call from her father, who has travelled out of town. He, too, decides to sing for his daughter. She chuckles as he sings the second stanza;

"*How old are you now? How old are you now? How old are you now, Rachel? How old are you now?*"

"*I'm 32 years today, I'm 32 years today, I'm 32 years today...ay...aaayyy. I'm 32 years to-day!*"

"*We wish you...*" he continues as she beams.

"Thank you, Daddy! I love you!"

"I love you too, Rache! Have a great birthday."

Rachel sighs when they disconnect. Her father can be so sweet at times. Rachel wonders if she and her step-mother will ever be so close. *If only…*

After her devotional time, she goes down to the kitchen to get some breakfast and receives more birthday greetings from their domestic staff. She smiles and giggles, responding in thanks and amen, as appropriate. She has a quick breakfast of cereal, before returning to her room to get ready for the day.

***

Rachel exits the bathroom just as her phone rings. She quickly dries her hands before going to pick the call. She smiles when she sees the caller ID.

"Hi," she answers.

"Happy Birthday, Rachel." Ejike's voice sounds rich and smooth like velvet.

Rachel feels a drug stimulating her nervous system, causing her to smile uncontrollably. "Thanks, Ejike," she breathes, as her heart pounds in her chest. She feels the need to take a seat, and she does on the bed.

"How are you today?"

"I'm good. How are you?"

"I'm great. I really wish I could come for your event today…"

"Oh, it's no problem…"

"Or just to see you," he says, pausing as he listens to her breathing over the phone. "I would have loved to take you out to celebrate."

Rachel swallows. "Hmmm…" She lets out a breath. "It would have been nice."

Ejike can hear the smile in her voice, and it causes him to giggle nervously. "Oh, cool. Then I owe you one… When next I'm in town."

"Sure…"

"How's next weekend?"

Is this really happening?! Am I really saying 'yes' to a date with Ejike…? I don't even know if he believes in God!

"Ummm… What, do you mean like a date?"

"Well… Yes, I suppose…" he replies, hesitantly. "Or just in-laws hanging out…" he quickly adds.

Rachel's quiet. She wants this too much. She doesn't even want to hear from God about it. *This guy is no good for me*, she suddenly concludes. "Ummm… I… I… Can't. I'm sorry."

"Don't be sorry. Just know that, if you ever need someone to talk to or to take you out, I'm here for you."

She swallows. "Thanks, Ejike. I appreciate your friendship."

"Alright! Have a good day, Rachel."

The line cuts before she can say "You too." He's upset, she thinks. But now she knows that she too weighs on his mind. *But if he doesn't love Jesus, he cannot love me*, she reasons, consoling herself in her decision to keep their relationship cordial.

***

A little girl, with pink ribbons in her hair and a matching baby-pink dress, sits surrounded by old furry toys, arranged for a meeting. Rachel is fascinated by her, how she has created a world in which these toys have names and personalities; a world where she's in control. She watches as the little girl places a faded, broken tiara on a formerly white teddy bear and beams.

"That's Tara. We found her two years ago. She was lost and, till now, we haven't been able to track her parents. We think they're from Ghana. We don't even know how old she is…" Yetunde, the programme officer, says, observing Rachel's keen interest in the girl.

"That's so sad," Rachel says, as she scans the other children in the room. "Do parents ever come looking for their children?"

"Very rarely."

Rachel squats down and wiggles her fingers at the little girl, a bit nervous about getting too close for comfort for her. The girl looks up and reveals gaps in her teeth in a full smile.

"I think she likes you," Yetunde says.

"What's the adoption process? I mean, are the children up for adoption?" Rachel asks, still squatting, as she plays with a brown bear.

"Yes, but let's talk about that in my office."

"Sure," Rachel replies, rising up. "I'd definitely like to talk to you about that later. But, can we play with the kids for a while, before we go? I was thinking we could dance, like have a mini party."

"No problem! As long as the music is wholesome," Yetunde replies, with a giggle.

"I'm on it!" Doug chimes in, making a selection on his mobile phone. Moments later, his Bluetooth portable speaker booms to life.

***

There's a young boy dancing in front of Rachel, who appears to be in his early teens. He clearly loves to dance and is an excellent stepper too. Even with his precise moves he is still quick to stop and grab a chair when the DJ – Rachel's friend Bose – hits pause on the track. Rachel almost missed the beat last time, as she admired his moves. But she knows how to cheat on this game and, besides, it's her birthday, so few are ready to challenge her for a seat.

But there are just three seats left, and four dancers in play. Two kids and two adults. Rachel is reminded to keep it moving when Doug bumps into her from the back. She laughs at his attempts to secure the closest available seat. He is definitely a worse, scandalous cheater! He dances with his butt as close to the chair as possible, and Rachel can't help laughing at the way he's moving his hands from side to side.

She doesn't respond fast enough when the room is met with sudden silence, then commotion, as the other dancers scramble to sit down! *Oh no!* She's out! Rachel laughs as she leaves the dance floor.

The music resumes, and the only girl left in the competition grabs her attention. Rachel instantly roots for her, chanting her name with the other residents and visitors, as Princess dances as if there's a trophy to be won. She's a really good dancer, although she has clearly picked up some bad moves from exposure to adult music videos. When the music stops, she's unchallenged, while Doug and the teenage boy fight over the second chair.

Doug clearly had the seat, but Rachel is happy to see him stumble and fall, so that the kid could secure his place in the finals. He dramatically raises his legs, and the children laugh at his fall. He gets up and dusts himself off, as he leaves the dance floor for the final show down.

"Nice fall!" Rachel chuckles.

"These kids play hardball!" he replies, giggling.

"Thanks for coming," Rachel turns to him to say sincerely. "And for everything you've done."

"It's been my pleasure!"

They return their gazes to the children still dancing their hearts out. It's going to be a tough one! Both of them are amazing dancers… But who's quickest?

"I really want Princess to win!" Rachel admits.

"So do I, 'cause she's a better dancer. But this isn't really a dancing competition…" Doug replies.

In that instant, Bose stops the track and one kid is left standing while the other has secured the last remaining seat. Princess shows maturity beyond her years when she laughs instead of cries at the proclamation that Tunde has won the musical chairs competition. However, both children are presented with prizes and given hugs by Rachel. They also take a nice photo together.

The last item of the day is to cut the birthday cake and present the gifts Rachel and her friends brought for the children and the orphanage.

***

At 8 pm on a Saturday night, Rachel's tired enough to go to bed. It has been an awesome day. After the outing to the orphanage in the late-morning till afternoon, she'd gone to the radio station to share cake with her colleagues, and also to host her show. She'd gotten more well-wishes and even birthday presents. She also used the opportunity on-air to thank all her friends who had given towards and accompanied her for the visit to the orphanage that day.

She'd gotten home at 7 pm and had her dinner. She knew she'd have to stay up a little later, to let the food digest some. So, after having a shower, she decided to relax to a good book on the sofa in the lounge she'd shared with Rochelle, that is now private to her.

The ringing of her phone now is an unwelcome distraction. She was already getting into the book. But today's still her birthday, and she has to be ready to welcome calls right up to midnight, she thinks and sighs. However, she's surprised when she sees who's calling her.

"Hey, Doug... What's up?"

"Hey, Birthday girl! How are you?"

"I'm good. Everything okay?"

"Yeah, sure. I just thought it would be nice to call and check on you. I hope you had a really good day today."

Rachel beams. "Yeah... You were there! And it was awesome. Thanks, again!"

"No wahala!" Doug smiles. He lets out a sigh. "So, what are you doing now?"

"Ummm... I'm just reading." Rachel yawns. "Feeling sleepy actually."

"Already?"

"Yeah... I'm so tired! You know I went to work after, right?"

"Yeah, I heard your show... Nice one."

"Thanks! So, what are you doing?"

"Hmmm... Honestly? Just been thinking about you. I had so much fun today!"

Rachel smiles. "Yeah, me too. You were really good with the kids. I didn't know you were so playful." She giggles.

"Yeah, I love kids! And I felt sorry for them really. Childhood is something you can never get back but is also so fundamental to who we are..."

"True... You sound like you have a story to tell."

"Don't we all?" he sighs. "But one day, I'll tell you. If you'll tell me yours..."

Rachel takes a deep breath and swallows. "Deal!"

Doug smiles. "So, what's your book about?"

Rachel chuckles. "It's a girlie one... You won't like it."

"Try me!"

"Well, it's "How Sade Got Her Groove Back"."

"Wait, isn't there a movie called "How Stella Got Her Groove Back"?"

Rachel giggles. "Yes, but this is like the Christian, Naija version for singles!"

Doug's hearty laughter stirs up more giggles from Rachel. "You're kidding!"

"Nope. It's pretty good, though. She's basically been nursing a broken heart over some guy she was dating, who wasn't good for her. And now, she's learning to love herself again, and also discovering God too!"

"Hmmm... Sounds inspiring."

"Yeah, it is. It's something I can relate to as well..." Rachel lets out and then heaves a sigh.

"Someone broke your heart, right?"

"Hm hmm," she mutters.

"I knew there was some other reason why you are on this long sabbatical from relationships. You can't let fear take control of you, Rachel. It will never let go. You will just need to learn to live with it, in spite of it, until you don't feel it anymore. That's what it means to be courageous. We are all afraid."

"Hmmm… Deep!"

"And you know what the Bible says?"

"What?"

"Perfect love casts out all fear!"

"Hey, that's my line!" Rachel chuckles, and Doug laughs along.

"It's just the truth!" he sighs. "Anyway… Let me leave you with your book. I'll call you tomorrow."

"Okay. Thanks for the call. It was…inspiring."

"Anytime, Rache! Goodnight!"

CHAPTER EIGHT

The birds are chirping a bit loudly this morning. One has perched itself on the tree just outside Doug's room, chirping away, as if warning of some omen. Doug stirs and pulls another pillow over his head, as he tries to block out the sound and the Monday sun that has seeped through the curtains to zero in on his eye-lids.

His attempts to get back to sleep are permanently disrupted when his bedroom door suddenly flies opens with a careless bang. Doug groans and turns in his bed, knowing it was no strange activity, but the intentional rebuke of his host and flat mate, Nike. The sound of the door handle hitting against the wall is augmented by Nike's irritating voice…

"Abeg, e don do! Go find job! Or you think this is Big Brother House?!"

"Guy!" Doug groans.

"Don't 'guy' me, abeg. It's eight thirty in the morning! What are you still doing in bed?"

Doug stirs and stretches. "Chill, na! I have an interview today, but it's not till 10 am."

"With which company this time?"

"At Urban FM."

"What is the job?"

"They need a sound guy…"

"You are not a sound *engineer*!"

"I'm a producer, nau… Leave it, joor! Sebi na job?!"

"Eh… Well, you better get it, because you cannot keep staying here rent free! Some of us have to pay bills!"

"I hear… I hear…"

"Be saying "I hear… I hear…" Your eyes will open when you come back, and I've changed the locks!"

Doug pulls his face as Nike turns his back to head out. The next thing he hears is the sound of the front door clanging shut. *Fuck!!! Why is Nike being a bastard?!*

He slowly gets out of bed and goes to the bathroom across the hall to ease himself. From there, he wanders into the kitchen and opens the fridge to inspect it for food. One egg left and half a loaf of bread. That will work. He brings them out to make his breakfast.

As he eats his meal in front of the TV, thanks to PCHN for some light today, his phone rings. He stretches his hand to where it's charging to check the caller ID. It's not a call he wants to answer, so he leaves it ringing. The persistent caller calls a few more times, irritating Doug.

He carries his tray and dumps it in the sink, leaving pieces of bread still on his plate, before heading back to the bathroom to have his bath. As the shower runs hot, he brushes his teeth in front of the mirror, thinking about what he's going to do to keep busy today. He might as well pay a visit to the radio station. But Rachel's show isn't until the afternoon. He could arrive early and find out if they are still looking for a sound guy, like Dongjap had mentioned last time he was there.

Yeah… That's what he'd do, he decides. He rinses out his tooth brush, pulls off his boxers and enters the shower.

***

The sound of his alarm reminder pierces into his subconscious mind and draws Ejike into reality. It's time to get out of bed. He already knows the purpose of the alarm, which he'd set yesterday to ensure that he got up in time to prepare for his meeting with his supervisor at 11 am. He'd actually been awake since 5 am working on his project, but he was feeling in need of more sleep, so he'd returned to bed, knowing his alarm would wake him on time.

He turns and dismisses the alarm on his phone, before rising up in bed. His blinds are still shut, so the room isn't overly bright for 8 am. He stretches and goes to ease himself in the bathroom attached to his bedroom. After washing his hands, he returns to his bedroom and switches on the light. He lets out a sigh as his eyes adjust to the brightness.

"Good morning, Lord," he mutters, as he wanders to the dressing table, where he'd kept his Bible.

At the corner of his bed, he kneels and prays, thanking God for the day. He opens his Bible to continue his daily readings. It's a habit he started about nine months ago, when he'd finally surrendered his life to Christ. He is now at the book of Philippians, and is finding his Bible reading journey enlightening. His memory verse today is the popular Philippians 4:13 – "*I can do all things through Him who gives me strength*" (NIV).

It is indeed a timely encouragement. His PhD research is trying, to say the least. He often wonders how he would have coped if he wasn't so fortunate. He knew so many people who had dropped out after their first year, because the work was too much and/or their funding was insufficient. He'd decided to offer one of his fellow students a room in his condo, last year. It was this friend and roommate whose influence led him to the Lord's feet.

Seto was not from a privileged background like Ejike, but he was extremely bright. However, even though his studies were funded by a scholarship, he still lived like a peasant because he sent as much money as he could back home to his family. When his mother took ill last year, and he couldn't meet up with her medical bills as well as rent, Ejike had offered him indefinite respite at his abode. He now saw it as a God-orchestrated event to bring him into the Kingdom, as so many other things changed for him then.

After his personal time, Ejike rises up and puts away his Bible. He heads over to his mini gym and starts the treadmill. After 15 minutes of running, he switches his equipment to work on his muscle strength for another 15 minutes. After his exercise regime, he returns to his room to shower and get dressed for the day.

At 9:30 am, he's enjoying a bowl of fruit, yoghurt, and cereal, while checking messages on his phone. There's a new message from Rachel on his WhatsApp.

"Thanks for your donation towards my birthday celebration last Saturday. It was a such a blessing. The children were really happy, and we had a great time with them. God bless you so much."

It seems so impersonal, like it is a broadcast, but she'd posted directly on their chat. He decides to reply.

"Hey, Rache. It was my pleasure. Good morning!"

***

Rachel smiles when she sees the reply from Ejike to the appreciation message she had sent to donors last night.

"Hi, Ejike. Good morning ☺" she types back.

The message delivers instantly, and she sees that he has received it when the two ticks turn blue. But then his 'online' status clears, suggesting that he had left their chat. She feels a bit disappointed, but decides to leave it alone.

She should start getting ready to go to the station. With her type of job, she can't afford to be late. Traffic is not even a decent excuse. She usually likes to get in an hour before time to prep and get in the right state of mind. They usually have meetings on Monday mornings too.

As she heads to her bedroom, her phone beeps again. She smiles, hoping it's a new message from Ejike. But it's just the daily devotional that Doug has been sending to her for months now. She doesn't usually read them, as she gets quite a number of devotional messages from friends, but she thinks she might just make an exception today.

Today's message is about being always ready to do God's will. Rachel feels encouraged by it and decides to respond to Doug this morning.

"*Thanks for this! I needed the reminder :) Good morning.*"

Instantly, his response comes. "*It's always my pleasure. I'm glad to know you're reading them too* 😊"

"*Yeah...*"

"*What time are you gonna be at the station today?*"

"*I should be there by 11 am. Why?*"

"*Just asking. I'll be there this morning too. Hopefully, we'll see before I leave...*"

"*Oh, okay.... What for?*"

"*I'm meeting with Dongjap about a few things.*"

"*Oh... Okay. See you later then.*"

Rachel wonders what the meeting with Dongjap could be about. Dj hadn't said anything to her about it. But then, he wasn't accountable to her. In fact, if anything, since Rochelle's wedding, Dongjap has been a little distant. Maybe she'd have a word with him today and see what's going on with him.

***

While still looking at the last message from Rachel, his phone rings. It's Ejike and Doug picks on the second ring.

"How nau?" he answers.

"I'm good. How are you, Doug?"

"I dey, o. I dey. What's up, nau?"

"It was Rachel's birthday on Saturday, wasn't it?"

"Yeah... It was. Did she call you to support?"

Ejike is silent as he considers Doug's question, which implies that he actually gave Rachel his number, and she chose not to contact him. "No, she didn't."

"Hmmm... She was probably busy with other things. But

I'm sure you can still send in your support. I'll send..."

"I already did."

"Oh... How?"

"Ekene gave me her number. So, I called her."

"Oh, okay. No problem, then..."

"You didn't give her my number, did you?"

"I'm sure I did. But I may have forgotten. It was a busy time."

Ejike gives a sad laugh. "So, have you guys been on a date yet?"

"Yeah, a couple of times..."

"I mean, like a real date? Cos, I got the impression that she's still single."

"Ejike... Lay off, alright? We don't all have money to throw around like you do. I like this girl... Can you just let me do my thing?"

"And what is that exactly?"

"Why don't you just watch and see?" Doug smirks.

"Hmmm... Well, I'm coming around this weekend. We'll see what's up, then. Take care of you."

Doug is stunned as he hears the disconnected signal. He looks at his mobile phone screen, which shows that the call with Ejike has ended. *WTF?! Did this dude just challenge me? Hmmm. We'll see alright!*

***

Rachel gets to the radio station just in time for their morning meeting at 11 am. Dongjap is already seated, and she's happy to see that there's an empty seat next to him. She goes to take it. He turns to greet her, and she knows now that something is definitely different between them.

"You okay?" she asks.

He nods in response, stoic.

"You don't seem fine."

"I am. Trust me. You okay?"

"Yes... Thanks," she sighs. "Can we talk later?"

Dongjap shrugs, just as a few more people enter the room with the Executive Director. Rachel sits back, feeling a little sad, as the Station Manager kicks off the meeting.

***

"So, your boyfriend showed up today…"

Rachel looks at Dongjap as if he's speaking a foreign language. "My *boyfriend*?"

"Yes. Doug," he says, folding his arms across his chest.

"He's not my boyfriend!"

Dongjap huffs. "Yeah… Keep telling yourself that."

"Is that what he told you? Is that why you're upset?"

"Look, who you date is your business. If you didn't like me, you should have just said so."

"Wait a minute… What's going on here? Why do you think I'm dating Doug?"

"I'm not blind. I was at your sister's wedding, and I saw you two. And then your birthday outing just confirmed my suspicions. It's alright. I'm not mad."

Rachel shakes her head, trying to understand Dongjap's summations and accusations. "Okay, well… Hmmm. Doug and I are just friends."

"Rachel, please. We're not kids. You can't seriously believe that nor expect others to believe there's nothing going on between you two," he said, looking at her intently. "Look, maybe you're not being honest with yourself. Whatever you do, open your eyes and make a choice about who you're spending your life with. Don't leave it to chance…because you'll regret it. I'm telling you as a friend. Because I care about you. Okay?"

"Okay. Thanks. And, ummm… I'm sorry if I made you feel bad or something. I didn't mean to. I'm just trying to figure out what I want, you know?"

"Yeah, I get it." He swallows.

"Friends?" she smiles, nervously.

"Always!" he beams, and they hug.

CHAPTER NINE

"*Hey… How was the meeting?*"

Rachel stares at the message from Doug on her phone. She's only just seeing it, though it was sent about 30 minutes ago. She has just a few minutes before her show starts. She wants to ignore the message, in light of all Dongjap has said, but she's curious about why he had come to her office today.

"*Hey… It was good. How are you?*"

"*I'm good. I'm sorry I couldn't stay. Dj said you guys had a meeting, so…*"

"*It's ok. No probs. So, how did your meeting with Dj go?*"

"*Cool… We can talk later tonight, when we see.*"

"*What's happening tonight?*"

"*The Love Feast at my church. I told you about it last week.*"

"*Oh, I forgot. I don't think I can come tonight.*"

"*Awww… Why?*"

"*I'm just…tired. I'm not really interested, to be honest.*"

"*Please come! It won't be the same without you! And Naden will be there…*"

"*Look, I'll talk to you later. I have to get ready for my show.*"

"*Aight, later! I'm listening as always* 😁"

Hmmm… Rachel thinks. *Would it really be so wrong to date Doug?* She'd never known anyone show as much humble determination to let her know she was special to him. And he clearly loved the things of God. What else did she want in a man? In a husband?

But there's no more time to ponder on that, as the intro to her radio session begins to play. It's show time!

***

"Hi, Rachel, I'm Dami from Ojota."

"Hi, Dami! Good to have you on the show. What would you like to **Ask Rachel**?"

"It's my boyfriend. We've been dating for six months, and I really love him. But he keeps pressuring me for sex. He says that I don't love him if I can't sleep with him. I don't know what to do… I don't want to lose him…"

"Oh, dear. I'm sorry you're in this situation. I can totally relate. But dear, this man doesn't love you."

"But he does! He is kind and sweet and is always thinking of me. I've never met someone who makes me feel as amazing as he does. It's just…this is his belief, you know? It's what he's used to."

"So, you do not believe the same things? He is not Christian?"

"Well, he is. He just doesn't believe that sex is off the table until marriage."

"And you believe that sex is off the table until marriage?"

"Yeah… I think so," she giggles nervously. "I'm not so strong again. I mean, we are going to get married… What should I do?"

"You should listen to your conscious and obey God. The Bible is very clear about the place of sex in marriage. Fornicators, those who have sex with people who are not their spouses, it says, will be judged! There's absolutely no justification for fornication, and I think your continued relationship with him is causing you to doubt God. You can't take man's word above God's. You can't serve God and your boyfriend. You have to choose your master."

"Okay... So, I'll tell him no, then."

"Sister, more than tell him no, you need to separate yourself from this person. The Bible asks, *"can two walk together unless they agree?"* This is just *one* doctrinal issue you disagree on. Are you saying you want to marry someone who you disagree with and whose leadership you cannot follow? Don't you know that a house divided against itself cannot stand?! That's why we are told very strongly not to be unequally yoked with unbelievers. Your boyfriend may say he believes, but it's one thing to say you believe with your mouth, it's another to *show* you believe with your actions and actually obey and submit to God. You really shouldn't be with someone who doesn't honour God's word – if you say you do."

"Okay, Rachel. I know what you're saying is right. I just pray for grace to obey. It's so hard."

"I know what you mean. I had such a painful experience myself. But we are the ones who put ourselves in such situations with our haste to be in a relationship, without first checking that the person we are getting involved with is going the same way we are. But a broken relationship or engagement is better than a failed marriage. Trust God to bring the best for you and wait for His peace... I know it's hard, but it's rewarding to be in the will of God. I'll pray for you too."

"Thank you! God bless you, Rachel."

"God bless you, too! Thanks again for calling in, Dami."

***

"OMG! This was your best show yet! I agree with you 100%. What fellowship has light to do with darkness? Spot on!"

Rachel smiles as she reads Doug's message on WhatsApp after her show.

"Thanks, Doug. I really appreciate the feedback."

"Seriously, Rache! My respect for you has just gone to another level. I don't know why you choose to hide behind the radio. People need to

hear these things, even in church!"

"Oh, no… I'm not cut out for that. This is my small ministry for now."

"And it will grow in Jesus' name!"

"Amen!" Rachel beams.

"Are you sure you don't want to come for the Love Feast tonight?"

Rachel leans back on her sofa and sighs. She really isn't doing anything. Sure, she isn't very good at socialising, but Doug makes up for where she lacks. She has never met someone so bold and confident, so free and yet so passionate for the things he believes in. *He believes in me and is a good friend to me. And honestly, I think I like him…*

"Sure, why not? Lol!"

"AWESOME! I can come get you…or we can meet there?"

"You can come…"

"Cool! See you soon 😁"

***

The room is filled with many smiling faces, some familiar but most are unfamiliar to Rachel. The smell of the different dishes and treats that have been brought together to make a visually stimulating spread fills the air, causing Rachel's tummy to growl. She and Doug had branched by a confectionary to buy some donuts as their contribution to the buffet. Rachel looks down at the peppered smoked chicken, wondering which angel brought this mouth-watering delight?

"OMG! Are you *the* Rachel Eden?!"

Rachel turns to look into the face of the excited young lady behind her in the queue to be served. She smiles at her question, nods and says, "Yes, that's me."

"Oh, wow! I love your show! I absolutely do!"

Rachel beams. "Thanks! That means a lot. Have you ever called in?"

"Oh, no. I'm not so bold. Maybe someday, sha," the lady giggles. "But thank you for what you are doing! God bless you!"

And without warning, the big fan dives in for a hug with the radio celebrity. Rachel responds by hugging her back. She sees Doug across the room smiling at her. The people around him are looking at her with strange recognition, respect, and awe. She's thinking they just found out that she's a Christian radio host/counsellor on Urban FM. She pulls from her hug and considers the woman before her.

"So, what's your name?"

"I'm Tokunbo."

"Nice to meet you, Tokunbo."

"I'm getting married soon." Tokunbo flashes her engagement ring at Rachel. "I'd really like to talk to you before then, if possible."

Rachel nods and brings out her phone. "Sure. Let's connect on WhatsApp."

Tokunbo beams and brings out her phone too.

***

"I can't believe you told all those people that I'm a radio personality!" Rachel protests on the drive back to her home.

"There's nothing wrong with someone else blowing your trumpet, dear! I'm very happy to be that someone!" Doug replies, giving her a quick side glance, before returning his gaze to the road.

Rachel lets out a huge sigh. "It felt good though."

"I bet!!! Do you know how many guys were asking me for your number?!"

They both laugh. "Seriously?" Rachel asks.

"Yes... As in... I had to tell them you were taken!"

"You did *what*?!"

"When it comes to you, Rache, I can't play fair..."

"So, you told them you were my *boyfriend*?!"

"No... Only that I want to be. It's the truth, Rachel. I'm not playing with you, Rache. I'm not in this relationship, this *friendship* for now... I'm in it for life."

Rachel is dumbfounded and speechless. She looks at

Doug as his Adam's apple bobs in his throat. Her eyes fall on his masculine features, his cleft jaw and thick arms, and she realises that she's attracted to him. She swallows and looks forward.

"I know I'm not rich like Ekene. And I'm not smooth like Ejike. But I'm real. With me, what you see is what you get…" he says, turning to her. He parks his car beside her parents' mansion. "What can I do to make you see that no other man can ever love you the way that I do?"

Rachel turns to Doug, tears gathering in her eyes. She doesn't know what to say. He reaches out to wipe a tear from her cheek.

"I know you're still unsure, but I'm crazy about you. Please just say you'll think about me… And pray about us."

Rachel nods and smiles. Doug smiles back and pulls her in for a hug.

"Let me walk you in…"

***

As soon as she gets in her bedroom, Rachel gets on her knees and prays to God about Doug and their evident relationship.

"God, I need Your help! I've done it my way before, and I don't want to make that mistake again. I honestly didn't set out to have a relationship with Doug, but it seems clear that we *do* have a relationship. I just want to know what sort of relationship it should be. Is Doug my husband?

"I've never looked at him that way. I have kept my heart from falling for him or anyone else, because I want to be led by You. But I know that I cannot be afraid to fall in love and to trust someone. And the more I know about Doug, the more I wonder if he could be the one You want for me.

"Please make Your will clear to me, so that I can move forward in peace or step back in confidence, knowing that You have someone better for me. Lord, please guide me, I pray in Jesus name. Amen!"

As she meditates, she recalls the scripture about Samuel and the sons of Jesse, and how Samuel had judged by their outward appearance and would have chosen wrongly, without God's guidance. She collects her NKJV Bible from the nightstand beside her bed and opens it to the book of First Samuel. Upon finding the correct chapter, she reads the story anew. Her eyes linger on these words in verse seven in Chapter 16: *"For the LORD does not see as man sees; for man looks at the outward appearance, but the LORD looks at the heart."*

The key is his heart, it dawns on Rachel. She recalls Jesus' words; *"Out of the depths of the heart, the mouth speaks."* He may not be rich, nor well-spoken nor even gorgeous to look at, but if he loves God, and he's sincere, that's what matters. He has shown me his heart. *The least I can do is give him a chance to prove himself*, Rachel surmises. She smiles thinking she knows what she will do and has been led by God in this decision.

"Thank You, God, for Your wisdom and counsel. I don't want to judge Doug by his outward presentation but by the things only You can see, hidden in his heart. I want to know him more so that I can make the right decision about being with him. Please direct my paths and help me to be responsive to Your guidance in our relationship. Ultimately, it is You I trust, and I know You will never lead me astray.

"Thank You for Jesus, for salvation, for grace and for love. Thank You for all the ways You've blessed me. Please help me to continue to use my gifts to bless others in need, to the glory of Your name alone. Amen!"

CHAPTER TEN

The days after are surprisingly quiet. It's the longest Rachel has been without hearing from Doug, since the day they met, and she's actually concerned. She soon realises that she's missing his constant attention. Apart from the devotional messages that he still sends daily, which she has been reading more of lately, they haven't really been exchanging messages.

She wonders maybe he's expecting her to get back to him about his request, but she doesn't quite know what she would say. Especially now that he has let the silence between them drag out for four days! Is he upset? Or has he changed his mind and decided she isn't worth the effort after all? She doesn't feel good about the possibility of either.

Today, she decides to send a response to his devotional post, hoping for some interaction.

"This was inspiring, thanks!"

She's not sure what to make of his response, *"Yw"*. Basically, *"you're welcome, but I really can't be bothered to chat with you…"* she translates. *Ok-ay!*

She puts her phone away, deciding to let it be. Wasn't today's message titled: *"Peace, Be Still"*? She would surely hold her peace.

***

Doug knows that he should have sent Rachel a better response, but he's honestly too stressed out. This week hasn't been going his way at all! First, Nike issues threats of eviction, and then he crashes into another driver on his way back home, after dropping Rachel on Monday night.

Fortunately, the other driver's car wasn't as badly damaged, and he managed to level all the blame on him, so the man felt guilty and agreed to pay for the repair work on both cars. The car, which actually belongs to Ejike, has been at the mechanic all week, and he's been so badly inconvenienced. To make matters worse, Ejike called him, because the other man's insurance company had called him, being the owner of the vehicle, to ask him about the accident. To say he was mad is putting it lightly.

"*Why didn't you tell me?!*" he had fumed.

"*There was no need. I had it handled. I don't even know why they called you.*"

"*You're unbelievable, Doug! I can't believe how selfish you are!*"

"*Haba! It was just a small accident… The damage wasn't even that bad.*"

"*Eh, no problem! Just give me my key when I come on Saturday. I should have taken it back ages ago.*"

"*But you're not even using the car! You're in Port Harcourt for God's sake!*"

"*I'd rather have it sitting in the garage, where it's safe, than have someone as ungrateful and reckless as you driving it!*"

"*This is about Rachel, isn't it?*"

"*What???!*"

"*You're just jealous that she's with me and not you.*"

"*You know what, Doug, you need help! Take it easy.*"

Now he's without a car, without a job, and almost without a home, he's feeling quite desperate. He still has a few friends with resources at his disposal. The problem is figuring out the next most strategic survival move…

***

"You're tuned in to 94.2 Urban FM! I'm still your host, Rachel Eden, and I'm taking questions about relationships, love, and marriage. Caller on line 2, where you calling from?"

"Hi, Rache. This is Doug from Ebute Metta."

Rachel is still upon recognising Doug's voice. Her heart races as she wonders what he could be calling about. She soon catches herself and resumes her professionalism.

"Hi, Doug! Thanks for calling in! What would you like to **Ask Rachel?**"

"There's this lady I met some months ago. She's totally out of my league. She's beautiful, well-educated, and from a wealthy background, but she's so unbelievably humble. I've completely fallen in love with her, and I've tried to tell her that I want to be her man. Do you have any tips for how I can win her heart?"

Rachel swallows, being both flattered and flustered by his declaration. "Well, you said she's humble, right…"

"Very."

"Then she's probably not about the superficial things. Show her that you are someone she can depend on and trust, because every woman needs that security. And when the time is right, don't be afraid to ask her straight up. If she turns you down, at least you'd know you tried."

"Thanks, Rachel! You're really so wise! Can I ask you another question?"

"Sure."

"Will you go on a date with me tonight?"

The air is still, and the question hangs. This is not the right time nor place, Rachel thinks. But it is sort of romantic, and she feels she already knows the answer to the question. She truly wants to, and needs to, know this man more.

She takes in a deep breath and says, "Yes."

"Really?!" Doug exclaims.

Rachel laughs, especially as Dongjap has decided to take

over and is now playing a Nigerian romantic classic over the airwaves. "Yes," she says again. "Thanks for calling in, Doug! Oh my... I think we're ready for another break!"

2face Idibia's melodic tune "African Queen" plays in the background as Rachel shuts her eyes, feeling a need to pray.

***

"I knew it! I just knew there was something between you two!" Bose says excitedly on the phone to Rachel. "Oh, but that was really romantic, Rache. You'll tell me how it goes tonight, won't you?"

"Yeah, I will. Honestly, I'm not really nervous like I thought I would be when I start dating again, cause he's my friend, y'know? It's like I'm going out with my friend, and we're hanging out."

"Yeah, but you want it to be romantic too, nau! It can't be just 'friendly', 'cause you might as well leave him in the friendzone. There has to be chemistry!"

"Yeah... Well, I like him. I think he's cute."

"Yeah, he is. I'm happy for you, girl! You're finally getting back on the horse!" Bose laughs aloud.

Rachel giggles. "I guess... Let's see how it goes. How are you and Nonye?"

"We're good. He should be around this weekend. Maybe we can double-date?"

"Abeg, slow your roll. Let me do the first date first!" They both laugh. "Thanks for calling, dear."

"No mention! I'll call later for the gist. Enjoy your date!"

"Thanks, girl! Later."

Rachel sighs as she puts her phone down. It feels good to have Bose's positivity and assurance. She had met Doug on her birthday outing and had only nice things to say about him afterwards.

"He seems like a nice guy..."
"Oh, he's funny!"
"Awww... So sweet!"

"*He's so into you!*"

Rachel remembers a few of the things Bose had whispered to her throughout the day. Though they were not best friends, they were old friends, who recently reconnected and were making the effort to be in each other's lives. Rachel had found that life had caused many of her friendships to fizzle to acquaintances, especially with many getting married, having children, relocating or simply trying to climb that career ladder. She had just a handful of people she still spoke with regularly, and Bose was one of the closest. She often listened in to her show and gave Rachel feedback, something that bonded them ever closer.

Rachel smiles, remembering the things Doug had said about her today on the radio. He really was very sweet. She can see herself falling for him.

***

Rachel's almost ready when she hears Doug speaking to the steward downstairs. She didn't hear his car drive into her compound, but decides she must have missed it. She takes a final look at her reflection and smiles, thinking she's looking good and very pretty in a stylish, blue, mid-length, fitted dress.

She leaves her room and heads down the grand stairway in her father's mansion. Doug comes into view with a smile on his face. He's wearing one of his smarter shirts that she has seen him wear before, over his worn, faded jeans. She thinks he could have made more of an effort, but she doesn't want to judge him by his appearance. She remembers what he said on Monday night; "*I know I'm not rich like Ekene. And I'm not smooth like Ejike. But I'm real. With me, what you see is what you get...*" and she smiles.

With Doug, there's no pretence. No forming. He's just who he is. A simple guy. A sincere man, and that's good enough for her.

"You look beautiful," he says, when she reaches the last

step, and he extends his hand to assist her off it. "I feel lucky!"

She beams. "Thanks!"

He pulls her in for a holy hug; a hug free from any sexual or sensual meaning. Just nice. And then he takes a hold of her hand. He has big, firm hands with thick long fingers. She likes the way her hands fit perfectly into his.

As they walk out of her home, he says, "I'm sorry, my car developed a fault today, so it's in the workshop. I hope you don't mind if we use yours? Or if you'd prefer, I could call an Uber?"

"No, it's okay," Rachel looks at him and smiles. "We can take my car. But you're driving!"

Doug beams. "No problem."

***

As they ride to their destination, Rachel is thinking about how strange this week has been for them, with him not really calling nor chatting with her as much. She decides to ask him how his week has been.

"Honestly, it's been a bit stressful. I'm sorry that I haven't been myself. I missed you, though…"

She smiles at his assurance. "Yeah. I missed you too," she confesses.

He turns and grins at her. "Well, I'm with you now. I feel so much better."

Awww, how romantic! She swallows and observes the road as he drives. It's his turn to ask about her week.

"It was good. Same ol' same ol', really."

"And your show?"

"It's been good, as usual. I really love talking about my Faith and counselling people about relationships, so it's great that it's my job too."

"Yeah, you're awesome! You're destined for great things, babe!"

"Thank you!" she replies and sighs.

Doug turns into the driveway, when they reach their destination. It's a Restaurant and Bar, with an outdoor Suya Spot, on one of the inner streets of Lekki Phase 1. Rachel has never been there before and takes in her surroundings.

Doug leads the way to settle in the outdoor sitting area, where there's a two-seater sofa, a long coffee table and a canopy. It looks and feels cosy, but yet casual. She takes a seat on the sofa when Doug directs her to, and then he settles down beside her.

"Hmmm… This is nice," Rachel mutters. "What do they serve here?"

"Anything you want. It's pretty intercontinental. But they have the best suya in Lagos! I thought we could have that with chips or something."

Rachel nods. She could go for suya. The smell of the spicy grilled meat is already taking over her senses. "Sounds good."

Doug bobs his head and then signals for a waiter to come and take their order.

***

It was a lovely evening, Rachel thinks, as Doug drives her back home. The air was cool and refreshing, their conversation flowed easily and naturally. Doug made her laugh with his endless stories about his experiences in Lagos. They didn't really talk about themselves so much, as expected on a first date. She considers that they already know a lot of the basic things; like what they do, where they live and what they believe about God and Jesus. There'll be time for some more deep talk later, Rachel opines to herself.

Doug presses the horn when they arrive at the gates to her family home. He drives in and parks her car expertly. Then he escorts her to her front door, like a gentleman.

"Goodnight, Rachel. I really had a great time with you, tonight."

She smiles and wonders nervously, if he will try to kiss her.

"Goodnight..." she breathes. "I had fun."

He's still holding her hand and affectionately rubs it. He lifts it to his lips and places a kiss on it. "See you tomorrow."

"Okay," she replies, with longing. She sighs and turns to enter her home. *That was sweet*, she thinks.

She smiles as she goes up to her room. She hears the front door open and shut again, and decides to look out of her window when she gets to her room. It has a view of the driveway, the gate, and the street. The steward is returning to the house, and Doug is walking away with what looks like a doggy bag. *Hmmm...*

He doesn't enter an Uber when he leaves her home, as she'd expected. Rather, he hails an okada rider, and she watches as he expertly sets himself on it, and they ride away. She shouldn't think anything of it. It doesn't mean anything.

Instead, she begins to change into her nightwear and thinks about what a lovely first date she just had with Doug.

CHAPTER ELEVEN

"Good morning, beautiful."

Rachel wakes up to a message from Doug on her WhatsApp. She smiles, thinking he's officially her boyfriend now. *I've got a boyfriend!*

"Good morning 😊 How was your night?" she sends back.

"It was good. I had the best evening 😁!"

"LOL!"

"What are you doing today?"

"There's a programme at my church this afternoon. I'm speaking…"

"Oh, nice! What about? Am I invited?"

"Sure, why not? It's for singles, actually. I don't know how I forgot to mention it yesterday."

"No problem. What time is it?"

"It starts at 1 pm, but I plan to be there by twelve thirty."

"Cool. I'll come over this morning, so we can hang out before then…"

"That'll be nice. See you later."

"😁"

Rachel beams. She rises from bed to pray and get the day started off right.

THE NAIVE WIFE: RACHEL'S CHOICE

***

When Doug arrives at her doorstep today, there's a different energy between them. He doesn't hesitate to take her in his arms and wrap her in a warm embrace. She enjoys the fact that it's longer than their previous hugs. He also smells good, she thinks.

Immediately, he holds her hand, and they walk into her house together. They settle comfortably on the settee in the exquisite living area downstairs, where the family members entertain their guests. Doug feels right at home already, as he goes to collect the remote control and changes the channel to a sports station. He extends his hand to Rachel and pulls her close to him, so that she's leaning on him on the sofa.

She likes the feel of his chest and relaxes against him, as they cuddle on the sofa. She's thinking how comfortable they are with each other, when he asks, "Have you had breakfast?"

"Yeah... Have you?"

"Didn't really have time. What is there to eat?"

"Let me go check," Rachel rises up, feeling silly for not having thought to offer him food. "Do you want anything in particular?"

"Ummm... Plantain and egg sounds good. With peppers, tomatoes and onions! Not too oily, please... I'm watching my weight," he adds.

Hmmm... Rachel can't help thinking that he is quite particular when it comes to his food. She passes his message across to the steward when she gets in the kitchen, and returns with a tray containing a carton of orange juice and two glasses.

Doug beams when he sees her initiative and thanks her for the drink. They soon settle back into their cuddle and continue to watch the TV screen.

***

It's 12 pm, and Rachel's almost ready to go to the church. Doug is watching a programme on Africa Magic, when she returns from changing in her bedroom. The doorbell sounds and she goes to get it.

She's stunned to see the handsome man at the door. In fact, he takes her breath away, and she has to catch herself from staring into his dark eyes. She's suddenly happy that she's all dressed up to go out and looking her best.

"Hi, Rachel… I'm sorry, I know I should have called," Ejike says.

She swallows. "Oh, no problem. Come in!"

Ejike steps into the house, his heart racing in his chest. Rachel looks amazing as always, but somehow, he'd underestimated the impact of seeing her again. He hears someone approaching and soon spots Doug. He freezes when their eyes meet.

"Hey, Ejike," Doug says, a slight smirk on his face. He takes Rachel by her waist, stating his claim, when she comes near to him. "What you doing here?"

Ejike is speechless. He's too late. Or is this just a misunderstanding? He swallows.

"I'm in town, and I thought to say hello…" He looks at Rachel, hoping she'd pull away from Doug, the way she used to. Hoping she'd save him from the great embarrassment he is feeling, showing up at her door unannounced, to find her with another man.

But she doesn't. Yes, she looks uncomfortable, but she doesn't attempt to correct the impression that Doug is giving, which is that they are dating.

Rachel's heart is beating fast. Her attraction to Ejike is so strong. But she thinks that's all it is. Sexual attraction. Like Eliab, he is beautiful to behold. He's the kind of man women would throw themselves at. And the kind likely to accept all advances and take at his will.

She reasons that this is the man she should be weary of. It was for him that she'd been forewarned of God to not *"consider his appearance or his height, for I have rejected him"*.

"I wish you'd called or sent a message. We're just heading to church."

Doug beams at Rachel and returns a victorious grin to Ejike. *She's mine!*

"Sure. My bad," Ejike mutters, turning back to the door.

"Here… Let me escort you out," Doug says, as he follows Ejike, leaving Rachel looking after both of them.

***

"So, you're dating…" Ejike acknowledges the evidence.

"Look, Ejike… I know you like her too, but you can get any girl you want. We both know it's not the same with me. And I *really* like her."

Ejike simply nods.

"I'm sorry about your car, mehn. I really am. And for not telling you about the accident. I just thought I could fix it first."

"It's okay. I forgive you."

Doug hugs Ejike. "Thanks, man! So, can I keep the key?"

"Nope," Ejike says. Doug's expression changes, and Ejike's sad. He was just apologising to have his way. Too bad for him. "Where's the car?"

Doug walks away and shouts, "I'll send you the address to pick it up. Later!"

***

"I'll let you all know now that I'm a Feminist. I believe in the equality of the sexes. I believe that gender is a social construction that oppresses both men and women, through the roles, expectations, and limitations we assign to them," Rachel says to the congregation as she gives her talk on 'Leadership in Marriage'. She looks across the bewildered congregation and continues. "But, before I am a Feminist, I am a Christian. Before I am a woman, I am a child of God! My first identity is in the relationship I have with my Father, and it is His wisdom that I choose to submit to. In any way Feminism contradicts God's word, I must exalt the Word of

God. And the Word tells me that the man is the head of the home."

An applause rings out in the congregation. Rachel smiles. "Leadership in marriage is about submission to God and not to man, because marriage is God's design. The husband has been appointed the head as part of a divine order, and while that is a great responsibility for him, it is also greatly humbling for the wife, who is called to honour him and submit to his leadership. It is not easy for either the man nor the woman, but someone has to lead; someone has to take that responsibility, and the mantle has been given to husbands. We should not frustrate them in this but support them. Help them by showing our loyalty and faith in their ability."

Doug is pleased about the message Rachel is preaching. He's happy to know that she would be a submissive and supportive wife. But is she any good in the kitchen, he wonders?

He is yet to sample her cooking. But knowing her privileged background, they might simply employ a cook when they get married. And that's fine with him. He smiles and claps along with the congregation as she continues her ministration.

***

The speakers at the conference are each given a special take-away pack, while the attendees have only small chops. Doug shares his puff-puff with Rachel as she drives to the radio station, for her Saturday show. He longs for the food in her pack, which she's yet to touch.

"You're going to eat that?" he finally asks.

She looks over at the goodie bag and nods. "Yeah, but you can have some."

"Thanks! I'll just take a little."

"Or you can just finish it," she says on second thought. He seems pretty hungry, and she would be fine until later.

"Ok, thanks!"

Before they reach their destination, the take-away pack of jollof rice, turkey and plantain is consumed, and Doug smiles happily, now that he's satisfied.

"Hmmm... That was delicious!"

Rachel smiles at him as she pulls into her parking spot.

"So, when am I going to taste your cooking?" he asks, coming out of the car and going to hold her close, as they walk into the radio station.

She chuckles. "Who told you I cook?!"

"Correct woman like you?"

"I'm a Feminist, remember?"

"If I remember correctly, you're a Christian first."

She laughs out loud. "So, you were listening..."

"Always, baby!"

***

At the station, Doug greets everyone they pass and bumps fists with those who recognise him and must have listened to Rachel's show yesterday. He feels like a celebrity, dating the beautiful, eligible Rachel Eden.

When they get to her studio, another radio host is still on seat. Dongjap greets Rachel and shakes hands with Doug. Rachel sits and goes over her plan for today's show. Doug is on his phone. She thinks it's sweet that he wants to and has decided to spend the day with her.

She soon remembers something he had promised to discuss with her but had obviously forgotten about. "So, you never told me what you came to see Dongjap about..."

Doug doesn't appear to have heard her.

"Doug?"

He looks up and at her, raising his brows. "What?"

"What was your meeting with Dongjap about on Monday?"

"Oh," he says. "You're still on that? I just needed a favour..."

"What kind? I hope it's not private. If it's none of my business…"

He turns and looks at her, thinking he might as well give her an answer. "I have an idea for a show… I thought he could help me pitch it or something."

"Oh, really? But you never told me."

He shrugs. "Would you be able to help?"

"I don't know. I could try…"

He's excited at the prospect. "Really?"

"Yeah… Maybe. You never know."

"Let me think more on it and share with you later, okay? I want you to really get it."

She nods. "Sure! I'll be happy to help."

He reaches out and squeezes her hand. "You're amazing. Thanks!"

***

"So, tell me about your family…" Rachel asks.

They are back at her home and are now in the private lounge upstairs, eating dinner. The cook had prepared egusi soup, with goat meat and swallow. Doug requested for poundo yam, while Rachel chose semolina. She feels so free to eat this traditional meal with him, with her bare hands and giggles when he licks his fingers.

"What do you want to know?" he replies.

"I don't know… Where are they? How many siblings do you have? Are your parents still alive? Together? I just don't know any of these things about you…"

Doug swallows some food and looks at Rachel. He pulls a smile on his face. "I don't really have a close family. My parents separated when I was young. I was their only child. They both married again and had other kids, and we're grown now."

"Okay… Hmmm. Well, I'm an only child of my parents too. But my mom's late. And they were never married."

"But at least you live with your dad, and he obviously loves you very much!"

"Yes, he does. I know our situations are quite different…"

"Very different," he interrupts. "I first ran away from home when I was ten. My mom's second husband was abusive, and he didn't like me."

"Oh, no! I'm so sorry," Rachel says.

Doug shrugs. "C'est la vie! That's why I don't like to talk about the past. Too much darkness. I like to stay positive and keep going and doing what makes me happy."

Rachel nods. "I get you. Life's too short, eh?"

"You know?!" he giggles.

"But, are you in touch with any of your family now?"

"Yeah… I keep in touch. I send my mom money sometimes, when I have it. I'm also staying with my cousin, her sister's son. So, I'm connected. Just not close."

"I get." She smiles at him and he smiles back. She returns to her meal, feeling like she finally knows him more and understands why he is the way he is. His story, though tragic, has endeared him to her. She really hopes he finds his happiness.

CHAPTER TWELVE

Three Months Later…

The mannequin dressed in a steel black suit set, standing at a shop window, catches Rachel's attention as she walks through the Palms Shopping Mall, in Lekki. The fit of the suit looks so elegant, she can just imagine Doug wearing it. *He would look amazing*, she thinks.

She walks into the shop to take a closer look and also have a feel of the fabric. *Hmmm… It's rich. How much?* She looks for the price tag.

"Can I help you, ma'am?" the store attendant asks, as she approaches Rachel.

"Yes, please. How much is this?"

"Let me have a look. I know it's one of our sale items. We don't have many left," the attendant replies. She pulls out a suit from the rack and checks the tag. "Yes, ma'am. The sale price for the set is N149,000."

Wow! That's much. Hmmm…

"Is it for your husband? He would love it, I'm sure."

"No. For my boyfriend. What's the biggest size you have? He's kinda tall and big built."

"Let me confirm that for you…" the attendant goes to the till to check the stocks.

Rachel's phone rings. She smiles on seeing the caller ID.

"Hey, babe. You here?" she answers.

"Yeah… Just parking. Where are you?"

"I'm just heading to the food court."

"I'll meet you there."

"Aight, babe."

The attendant returns and tells Rachel the sizes that they have available for the suit. Rachel takes another look at the mannequin. It would make a lovely Christmas gift, she decides.

"Okay, I'll get it. But please, wrap it quickly, as I'm supposed to be meeting him now."

"Sure, ma'am."

***

Rachel beams when she sees Doug approaching the food court. She goes to him and gives him a hug and a soft kiss on the lips. He smiles down at her and slides his hand down to hold hers, as they walk over to look at the food options at KFC.

"Have you bought the tickets?" Doug asks.

"Not yet. We still have time."

"Okay, no problem."

"How was your show today?" Rachel asks.

"It was great! The Christmas carols came together really well. They're going to do a repeat tomorrow morning."

"Congratulations, Mr Producer!" Rachel giggles.

"I couldn't have done it without you…" Doug grins and gives her a quick kiss.

They look up at the menu when they finally get to the front of the queue. They needn't have bothered. They end up ordering the same thing they always order.

"We'll have the Zinger burger meal, with extra chicken and fries. What are you drinking, babe?" Doug asks.

"I'll just have water, thanks."

"And I'll have Fanta."

The cashier punches in their order and calls the price. Doug pulls out his card and pays for their meal. When she leaves to pack their tray with the order, he turns to Rachel.

"So, what did you buy?"

"Ummm… Nothing much."

"That's quite a big bag," he grins.

"Richard asked me to pick something for him."

"Oh… Okay." He turns back to the cashier, who has now finished loading their tray. He carries it across to a table and settles into a seat. Rachel takes a seat across from him.

Doug's phone rings, and she watches as he answers the call. She grabs a piece of chicken and bites into it. It's spicy and succulent. She dips a chip in the ketchup bowl and pops it into her mouth, trying not to listen in to Doug's conversation.

He cuts it short and returns his attention to her. They smile lovingly at each other as they enjoy their meal.

***

The movie is a Christmas romantic comedy, and they arrive just as the credits begin, with an upbeat Christmas song. Rachel's happy that Doug allowed her to pick their movie today. She's come to know that he's generally not too fussy about anything but his meals. She's cooked for him a few times, and he seems to like her cooking.

The hall is packed and they manage to find a couple of empty seats somewhere in the middle. When they settle in their seats, Rachel leans into Doug and they lock hands, as the dialogue starts in the movie. Rachel smiles, feeling happy.

The movie is as funny as the trailers suggest, and the cinema hall bubbles continuously with laughter. Doug is enjoying himself, even though he thinks the film is a bit too cheesy. But nothing beats spending time with his girl. He rubs her arm fondly, and she turns up to him and smiles. They share a brief kiss, before returning their attention to the movie.

They are both smiling when the movie ends. It was another lovely evening for the couple, but the night is not over. They stroll hand in hand to the parking lot together.

They walk by Doug's parking spot, where Rachel's Toyota Prius sits pretty. She smiles every time she sees Doug squeeze himself into it. He'd asked to borrow her car once, a couple of months ago, but she needed it, so she offered him the use of her old Prius. He's been driving it ever since. Apparently, his Hyundai had been recalled for safety reasons, so he's now saving to buy a jeep.

They get to her 2010 Mazda 3 and kiss before they separate.

"Last person to the estate is a clown!" Doug jokes, as he races to get to his ride. Rachel laughs and quickly enters her car. She loves racing cars with Doug.

***

"Can I stay over tonight?"

They are in her bedroom, watching TV. The door is shut, and they are cuddled together on the bed. He's behind her, propped up by pillows, while she rests her head on his broad shoulders, their arms intertwined.

This is not the first time he's asked. And it won't be the first time he's slept over. The very first time, he didn't really ask. It just got so late that it didn't seem safe for him to drive across the Third Mainland Bridge to his home, especially as he'd complained about being harassed on the bridge at night before. So, she'd volunteered to make up Richard's old room for him.

He'd slept there a couple of times until Mrs Eden noticed and expressed her disagreement at them using Richard's room. After that, he'd tried to leave her home earlier to get home safe. When he didn't want to leave her, like tonight, he asked to sleep over.

She knew it wasn't a good arrangement. It didn't give anyone observing a good impression about her, as they must have assumed that they were having sex. But they were not. They just kissed and cuddled and sometimes fondled, when things got too heated. She didn't like to let him sleep over for that reason, even though they were both committed to keeping sex until marriage. But she also loved being with him and cuddling in his arms at night.

"It's Christmas Eve..." he continues. "Let's stay together, babe."

Hmmm... She lets out a sigh. By now, everyone, including her father, is aware that Doug sometimes sleeps over. What must they think of her? But what does it matter, when it's *her* relationship, and she knows that their motives are pure?

"Okay..." she says. "It's Christmas."

"Thanks, baby," he smiles, relaxing and giving her a kiss on her head. The sound of laughter from the TV show draws their attention back to it, and they resume their evening entertainment.

***

"Merry Christmas!" Doug says to a still sleepy Rachel. Her lips turn up in a smile as she looks at his radiant face. She notices that he's dressed ready to go. "I want to rush home and get a few things before we go to church today."

She nods. "Okay."

"Can we go to my church? Service is at 10 am today. We should be done by 12."

Rachel shrugs. "No problem. I'll be ready by 10."

"Aight, I'll come and get you, and we can go in your car."

Sometimes, the way he speaks, she is convinced the Prius has been sold to him. He often refers to it as "my car". It doesn't really bother her that he drives it. She prefers him using the car than hopping on and off public transport everywhere. She just still feels very much the owner of the Prius, especially having fond old memories of driving it.

After he leaves, she struggles to return to sleep. She eventually gets up to pray and read her Bible. The house is quiet, and she's able to hear the musical tunes of the Christmas lights, draped around the Christmas tree downstairs. It sets the tone for her worship this morning.

***

As per their family tradition, the Edens are hosting their friends and extended family, with a Christmas Day open house. A barbecue is set up by the outdoor swimming pool, and a buffet is arranged in the dining area. The indoor bar is stocked with wines, spirits and juices. A bartender, aka mixologist, has been employed to make cocktails to serve all their guests as they arrive.

They have gone all out this year with a Santa Claus Grotto in their garden for the little ones. Vendors are also catering for the kids with hot dogs, burgers, popcorn and ice cream. For music, a pianist is entertaining the guests with classic Christmas songs on the grand piano in the lobby. The ambiance is indeed festive.

Rochelle and Ekene arrive for the event sporting a baby bump proudly, to the delight of Mrs Eden. The couple are glowing with tangible joy as, everywhere they go, they are greeted with awe and jubilation. Rachel is just as thrilled when she sees her sister, and they hug warmly. Ekene extends a hand to Doug, who's by Rachel's side.

Doug takes it and greets, "Congrats, my man! Well played."

Ekene chuckles, his joy greater than his dislike of Doug. "Merry Christmas!"

Rachel hugs her brother-in-law. "Merry Christmas! Is Ejike coming?"

Ekene shrugs, feeling uncomfortable. He moves away, following his wife, who's gone to greet other family and friends. "I don't know. He might," he manages to respond before turning to greet other party guests.

Rachel's a bit surprised that she had not been able to keep herself from asking about Ejike. She now finds her eyes roaming the room for him and keeping a watch at the front door. Realising what she's doing, she quickly turns to her boyfriend, whose eyes are on her. He raises his lips in a slight smile. She returns a bigger one, assuring him, in case he saw more than she meant for him to see.

She soon spots Bose, who's just arriving with Nonye, and excuses herself to go and welcome them. Doug sips his drink, watching her. She returns shortly with Bose, who's ever cheerful. She introduces her boyfriend.

"Nice to meet you," Doug says, shaking hands with Nonye.

"Likewise," he replies.

"What do you want to eat, babe?" Bose asks Nonye.

He shrugs and quickly picks a cocktail from a tray being carried by a waiter in smart, black and white attire. "Anything."

Bose pulls Rachel along with her, and Doug shouts after them, "Bring small chops!" to which Rachel nods.

***

Ejike arrives at the Eden mansion with his parents. He hadn't intended to but had been compelled by his father to come, as they are now family. Upon entering the compound, his eyes search for Rachel, as his heart hangs in expectation, often skipping a beat, whenever a lady with her frame comes into view. He shouldn't have come, he thinks.

"Hey, you made it!" Ekene greets his older brother excitedly. The pair hug.

"Where's our wife?"

"She's with her mom. They went up to her room a while ago."

"Okay." He won't ask of Rachel.

He doesn't need to. She suddenly appears with the light of the sun, giggling happily with her friend. His eyes follow her as she makes her way across the room, carrying a plate of grilled meat and corn from the barbecue outside. When she hands the plate to a man and kisses his lips, Ejike is stirred back to reality. He swallows.

Ekene doesn't miss the scene that plays before him. He doesn't quite know what to say to his brother. He decides to break his news, hoping Ejike will be distracted and become happy too.

"We're pregnant!"

"Oh, wow! Congrats, bro!" And the plan works, as Ejike beams at and hugs his brother joyfully.

***

I should go and greet him, Rachel thinks, when she finally spots Ejike with his brother across the room. *But why should I?* She argues with herself. *It's only polite… Besides, it might mean something if you don't… No, I shouldn't. Okay, later, not right away. Jeez! You're supposed to be over him!*

"May I have everyone's attention, please?"

The message doesn't quite register with Rachel, though the room suddenly quietens, and the music changes to something slower and romantic. Rachel soon recognises the tune of Stevie Wonder's "For Your Love", playing on the piano. She is both surprised and amazed when, after the long intro, Doug begins to sing the beautiful song. And his voice is trained. But more powerful are the lyrics he sings. The room is captivated.

She's looking at him, wondering what he's doing, afraid that she knows, and thinking that, though she saw it coming, it's way too soon. She swallows and avoids the eyes of others. What should she do? What is happening?

Someone is holding her hand, and he's bent on one knee. He has a smile on his face, and a box open with a ring on his other hand. The ring has no glory, but she forces herself to hear his words.

"Rachel, since you came into my life, you've made me the happiest man in the world. My dream, my greatest desire, is to make you the happiest woman in the world. I love you so much, and there's nothing I will not do for you if you will give me the honour of becoming your husband…"

Rachel is shaking. She's thinking "No". She glimpses his old pair of loafers and thinks, *how can this man look after me?* But she remembers, "*Do not judge him by his appearance…*" A man of purpose does not always look the part; she knows as she considers how David must have looked to Samuel, the Prophet.

She swallows as she begins to nod. If she didn't plan on marrying him, why was she dating him? This is the noble thing to do, she reasons.

The sudden jubilation all around distracts her from the anguish within.

CHAPTER THIRTEEN

She said "Yes!" *Oh my God, she said "Yes!"* Doug jubilates, as he rises up from his bent position to take Rachel in his arms. He's getting married to this beautiful, amazing, generous and passionate woman. He beams as he faces her friends and family present. His life is about to change!

So many people approach the pair to express their approval, support and well wishes. Chief Eden looks especially happy at the turn of events. His beautiful daughter is finally getting married. He decides to raise a toast to the engaged couple.

"To marriage, family, and happiness!"

"Marriage, family, and happiness!" everyone repeats, as they clink their glasses joyously.

Rachel doesn't have a glass, and she's not looking around for one to toast nor to drink from. She's drowning in the sea of happy faces and the multitude of voices wishing her and Doug a happy life together and asking her questions. She doesn't understand the words. She doesn't understand anything that's happening. She's just feeling like she missed something, but isn't sure what.

"Are you okay?" someone asks. She looks at her friend, Bose. She doesn't know what to say. Bose hugs her. "I know, it must be overwhelming. But when it's love, it's love. I'm happy for you both."

But is this love? Rachel realises that *that* is the essential thing she's missing in this experience. The knowing that what she has with Doug is love. A love she cannot live without…

***

What is love? The question torments her, as the answer evades her. Love is not a feeling; she has heard many say. Love is an action. Love is what you do.

So, technically, if she does the right thing by Doug, does that mean she loves him? How is her love for Doug different from the love she would have for a friend, to whom she also does right? Are emotions really not important at all? Are there not different degrees of love? Does it not matter that she doesn't feel particularly passionate about this person she's planning to spend the rest of her life *loving*?

But she doesn't have the luxury of time to worry about this technicality, as wedding plans are already underway. Mrs Eden eagerly takes up the responsibility and duty of coordinating wedding plans. She calls in her contacts from her daughter's wedding in August to host another glorious party. The Edens are leaning on a wedding in June, next year. Doug's family is flexible.

Rachel thinks six months is too soon to marry, considering how short her relationship with Doug is, but she is discouraged from considering a longer engagement. The longer engagement may put a strain on their relationship, and Chief Eden thinks that he'll be in a better position to support Doug once he's officially family. Besides, Rachel has to consider the fact that she's 32 years old. If she wants to have more than one child, they need to start planning for them and trying to conceive sooner rather than later.

She decides that all they really need is pre-marital counselling. Hopefully, it will help her answer this festering question about love and emotions.

***

"God is love," the counsellor says.

"I know that. How does that answer the question of love in marriage?"

The counsellor nods and smiles and looks at the couple before him. "Well, we can only truly understand love when we know God. Love is what God does and what He calls us to do. The Apostle Paul said it very clearly in First Corinthians chapter thirteen. If you open your Bible, we can read it together…"

They open their Bibles, and the counsellor calls on Doug to read the definition of love contained therein.

"*If I speak in the tongues of men or of angels, but do not have love, I am only a resounding gong or a clanging cymbal,*" Doug begins from verse one. "*If I have the gift of prophecy and can fathom all mysteries and all knowledge, and if I have a faith that can move mountains, but do not have love, I am nothing.*"

"What version of the Bible is that?" the counsellor asks.

"NIV."

"Okay, continue to verse eight."

"Three. *If I give all I possess to the poor and give over my body to hardship that I may boast, but do not have love, I gain nothing.* Four. *Love is patient, love is kind. It does not envy, it does not boast, it is not proud.* Five. *It does not dishonour others, it is not self-seeking, it is not easily angered, it keeps no record of wrongs.* Six. *Love does not delight in evil but rejoices with the truth.* Seven. *It always protects, always trusts, always hopes, always perseveres.* Eight. *Love never fails. But where there are prophecies, they will cease; where there are tongues, they will be stilled; where there is knowledge, it will pass away.*"

"Does that answer your question about what love is in marriage, Rachel?" the counsellor asks.

"I guess," she swallows. "So, there is no romance in the definition of love?"

"Romance is also something you do to show someone that you love them and care for them. Even if the feelings are not there, doing something romantic for someone you care about can help the feelings to grow. So, the way I see it, romance is neither the beginning nor ending of love. It's just another expression of love, like kindness," Doug attempts to answer.

"Beautiful," the counsellor smiles at Doug's response.

Rachel considers him and his response, and it makes sense. It actually lightens the burden she feels about the absence of passion or spark in *their* expression of love. They are still building on a right foundation, as long as the foundation of their love and relationship is Christ. She smiles, feeling relieved.

There may not be butterflies in her tummy, nor sweaty palms and racing hearts between them, but they have peace and comfort and happiness. With Doug, she has a companion, who's quickly becoming her best friend, and with whom she feels at home. Suddenly getting married to him doesn't feel as wrong, awkward, or scary. It feels exciting, the way it should, because they are about to embark on an expedition of love.

"Thanks. That helped."

Doug beams and squeezes Rachel's hand, and they both look on at the counsellor for more guidance.

***

With that settled, Rachel allows herself to get swept up with the wedding plans. She visits different places with her mother and sister, as they choose the best reception venue. Once the venue is chosen, the date of the wedding is fixed. All other plans now revolve around that date.

Timelines are drawn for the traditional introduction, which is to precede the traditional marriage ceremony and white wedding. Mrs Eden plans an international trip to shop for the wedding dress and other garments, while Rachel and Doug plan their first trip to visit his hometown and meet his parents. The trip with Doug to Oyo state conjures both anxiety and exhilaration in Rachel. With the wedding in June, the shopping trip is slated for after Rachel meets her soon to be in-laws, in the New Year.

"There's no need to be nervous. They'll love you like I do," Doug assures her during their drive on the Lagos-Ibadan expressway.

Their first stop is to see his dad and his family at Iseyin, then they'd return to Ibadan and arrive at his mom's place in time for dinner. They would spend the night and leave early the next day for Lagos. However, upon getting to his father's home, they learn that he'd gone out for a stroll over a year ago and never returned. He left behind a young wife with four children and no livelihood. The really sad part is that they still live in expectation of his return.

Rachel's sad to see the malnourished children who are related by blood to Doug. How could his father just run out on them, without ever looking back, she wonders? Doug is eager to leave as soon as they arrive. But before they do, Rachel gives the young mother all the cash in her hand, wishing she could have given more. The woman is beyond thrilled and grateful for the gift.

They get to his mom's place in the mid-afternoon, and the house is full of family. Everyone's happy to see Doug and to meet his fiancée. They gather to ask them questions about their lives, living and working in the city. They are very impressed that Rachel's a radio host, and even more impressed to learn that Doug also produces shows for the station, and is now working on a couple of TV shows too.

Rachel learns more about Doug's family and siblings. She's surprised to learn that he's a twin, and had a twin sister who died when they were babies. It was one of the things that led to the break-up of his parents' marriage. He has siblings from his mother's two marriages since, totalling five siblings on his mother's side. Two have left home to work in the city and marry, leaving three with her and her husband in the village.

After pouring through his childhood pictures, Rachel later goes to see how she can be of assistance in the kitchen. Mrs Folusho has made edikaikong soup with amala, a meal Rachel is unfamiliar with. She helps out by setting up the table for dinner. Dinner is a pleasant time, filled with more questions and stories, this time of Rachel and her family. The conversations soon turn to Faith, and Rachel is pleased to see that they are all professing and practising Christians.

The night is long with heat and mosquitoes, but the friendly and happy environment makes it bearable. In the morning, the pair set off early to beat the traffic going into Lagos, feeling that much closer for the experience they've shared. The Folushos are definitely keen about the upcoming wedding and have even chosen the colours for their aso'ebi – Red and Yellow.

***

The five-day trip to Dubai is the longest time Rachel and Doug have been apart since they began their relationship. Rachel keenly communicates with Doug via WhatsApp to keep him abreast of their activities and also to know how he's getting on at his end. However, she soon realises that she doesn't miss him as much as she thought she would, and he doesn't seem to miss her at all.

In the evenings, when Ekene calls Rochelle, and Chief Eden calls Mrs Eden, Doug never calls. And whenever she calls, they barely speak for two minutes before they seem to run out of things to say. And the "I love you"s they exchange feel forced… She doesn't feel loved, like someone who is desired. Again, she wonders about this missing emotional element in their relationship. Will it always be this way? Should it ever be this way?

On her third day, she makes a point of not contacting him at all, even via WhatsApp. By the time he remembers to check in on her, it's already past 10 pm at night, and she's very upset with him.

"Hey, babe. How was your day?"

She looks at the message on her phone, angry at the words he'd chosen. *I'm not your babe! I don't feel like your babe. And what do you care about how my day was???*

After a while, she replies with, *"It was fine. Thanks."*

"Where did you go today? Did you get the fabric for our traditional?"

Rachel rolls her eyes. *"Not yet."*

"Okay. I also need some suit material. I think it'll be cheaper there."

This feels like a business chat, Rachel thinks. *"Okay, I'll see. Good night."*

"Are you okay?"

"I'm fine."

"Sorry, I didn't get in touch all day. It was really busy. I missed you tho :)"

"No problem. Talk to you tomorrow."

Rachel wipes her tears from her eyes. She doesn't know how to communicate the frustration she's feeling at his ignorance when it comes to romancing a lady. But the truth is, he wasn't always this detached. When he wanted her, she consumed his mind, and he sought her out always. Maybe he's feeling his work is done, and he's home free.

Well, this is not what I signed up for…

CHAPTER FOURTEEN

Doug seems to have gotten the message from their chat the night before and makes a point of calling Rachel the following morning. It does much to cool her rising irritation. She later reaches out to him with WhatsApp messages, sending pictures of fabrics for their traditional marriage ceremony and for his groomsmen's suits. He has decided to wear the suit she bought him for Christmas as his wedding attire for the white wedding. It would only need some minor adjustments; in case he puts on or loses weight by then.

The last two days in Dubai see them chatting more and generally communicating better. Rachel finds the perfect wedding dress, and a second dress she had first seen on Instagram. They also get lots of fabrics to sew for the upcoming celebrations and buy some jewellery for the special occasion, including two platinum, engraved wedding bands. The shopping trip is a success, and Rachel expresses her gratitude to Mrs Eden for organising it.

"You're welcome," she says when Rachel says "Thank you" for the umpteenth time.

***

Valentine's Day soon comes around and, with it, its expectations of romance. Rachel is no exception in this regard and is eager to be swept off her feet with thoughtful gifts and attention from Doug. The day looks promising when she receives a message from him early in the morning.

"*Happy Valentine's Day, Beautiful!*"

She beams on receiving it and replies, "*Happy Valentine's, Babe* 😊"

"*My friend's organising a Valentine's Party at Murphy's Plaza tonight. I thought it'd be nice for us to go…*"

"Hmmm… Sounds good," she replies. She'd been anticipating something more intimate and private, but a night out with other couples and friends didn't sound so bad. "*I'll invite Bose and Nonye.*"

"*Cool! The more the merrier. I'll pick you around 8 pm* 😊"

"*Ok* 😊"

***

"What's up, beautiful people?! Happy Valentine's Day! It's the day marked for lovers all around the world, but I want to know…what does Valentine's Day mean to you? Call in, and let's have a chat, make a song request or simply **Ask Rachel**. I'm Rachel Eden, your host on 94.2 Urban FM on this beautiful day…"

"Hi, Rachel! I'm Kenneth, from Jakande. Happy Valentine's Day!"

"Happy Valentine's Day, Kenneth! Do you have a song request?"

"Yes, I do but, first, I have a question."

"Shoot!"

"Is it really the thought that counts?"

"Wow! That sounds like a trick question," Rachel giggles happily.

"No, I'm serious. Do you women really mean what you say when you say that?"

"Okay, let me try and understand the context. Is this a specific issue with someone you know?"

"You see, my wife and I have been married a couple of years, and when we were dating, she used to say that a lot. She even said she'd rather have my company than to receive flowers and candy on Valentine's Day. So, last year, we went swimming at our sports club and went out for dinner at Bukka Hut after. But she was so unhappy, and accused me of not being romantic."

"Hmmm… I think your wife doesn't quite know how to communicate what she wants. Yes, it is the thought that counts and the quality time together that matters. It's not really about how much you spend or where you go but, Jesus rightly said, *"where your treasure is, there your heart will be."* The truth is that people spend money on the things they value, and special occasions such as this day, are for showing the ones we love how much they mean to us."

"Okay, well, I don't buy into the commercialism of Valentine's Day. For me, my money is my time, and my time is my money. When I'm spending time, I'm spending money, and I like to think that *I'm* the gift. That being with me is more satisfying than spending money on things that don't last."

"Very true, Kenneth. But when you celebrate a birthday, and your friends come over, some bring gifts; some more thoughtful than others, right? Do you feel they all made the same contribution to your day, given their means?"

"Well, the person who brings a gift has done more, especially if the gift has significance. But not everyone can afford a gift…"

"God alone knows what each person can afford and the true value of their time. There are those friends that come to eat, and their presence at your party isn't about celebrating you, but helping themselves. So, these things are hard to judge. We just have to ask ourselves if we gave OUR best. Like Abel, who was thoughtful with what he brought before the Lord, we will be rewarded with appreciation for our efforts. But if we just do the bare minimum or what we think we can get away with, we shouldn't be surprised if, even that, is rejected!"

"Hmmm… I get. I guess I better try this year. Thanks, Rachel."

"Thanks for calling in, Kenneth! Do you have a song for the Mrs?"

"Yes… She loves Timi Dakolo's "Iyawo Mi"."

"It's coming right up! This is for the lovers… You're still tuned in to 94.2 Urban FM with Rachel Eden."

***

It's 8:30pm, and Rachel's dressed waiting for Doug to show up for their outing today. So far, the day has been a major disappointment. Apart from his message in the morning, she hasn't heard from him all day. She'd also been calling to find out why he's late, but his phone has just been ringing. Their first Valentine's and she's already feeling like an old, neglected wife, Rachel thinks and sighs.

The car horn of her Toyota Prius sounds, announcing his arrival. He enters the compound and calls her phone. "I'm downstairs," he says when she picks up.

No "sorry, I'm late." No attempt to give an excuse or explanation. *"I'm downstairs", as if he isn't almost 45 minutes late,* Rachel fumes. She takes some deep breaths, deciding she shouldn't make a big deal out of it. At least he didn't forget Valentine's Day altogether. At least he didn't forget his plan to take her out. At least they still have a lovely evening ahead. *Calm down, it's not a big deal.*

She manages a smile when she gets to the car and slips into the passenger seat. "Sorry, I'm late, dear," he says, cooling her temper. "How was your day?"

"It was good, thanks. How was yours?"

"Busy. Been on the road all day. I'm hungry, mehn!" he sighs, as he pulls out of the drive into the street.

Rachel feels bad. Obviously, he's had a stressful day. And

she'd been quick to think he didn't care.

She extends her hand to rub his arm. "Sorry, babe. I'm sure we can get something to eat at Murphy's."

He turns to her and smiles. "Yeah. You look good, babe!"

She beams. *That's more like it.* "Thanks!"

***

"Are you going to sing?" Doug leans into Rachel and shouts in her ear. There's quite a crowd at Murphy's tonight, and the music is very loud.

"Yeah, maybe," she shouts back. How are they going to have a decent conversation in a place like this, she wonders?

"Okay… You should probably place your order now. I want to go and put my song on the list," he says, as he stands up to go to the tablet set up for taking Karaoke song requests.

Rachel just nods after him. She's watching the door for Bose and Nonye. Bose said they were looking for parking. A beautiful lady walks into the club, dressed tastefully in white and pink. As Rachel admires her, she notices there's a hand on a waist. She follows it to look at the man with the lady.

Her heart skips a beat on seeing Ejike, looking ever so handsome in a midnight-blue shirt and black jeans. So, he's seeing someone now. Or maybe this is just one of his conquests… She forces herself to look away from the enviable couple.

Doug soon returns to their table. "Hey, you alright?" he asks.

"I'm fine." She stands up. "Let me pick my song."

"Sure…" Doug says. "What are you going to drink?"

"Chapman, please," she replies quickly.

She notices Ejike and his date as they settle into a corner of the club. He's being very gentlemanly with her, she notices. A waiter arrives at their table to take their orders. Rachel looks away and focuses on the song menu. She types

"Whitney", hoping to sing a couple of the music legend's songs…if she can still stomach it tonight.

After selecting "All The Man That I Need" and "I'm Your Baby, Tonight", she turns to return to her table. She can't help but look again at Ejike's table. She's shocked to catch his gaze. Like a deer caught in the lights, she freezes. But it's like he never saw her, because he soon turns away to laugh at something his date has said. The spell is broken, and Rachel manages to move her legs again.

"Hey, Rache!"

She turns in the direction of the call. It's Bose. She smiles in relief, trying to ignore the faint disappointment she feels that it wasn't Ejike calling her name.

"Hey dear! It took you long enough!" she says, as they hug.

"Parking around here is horrendous. Where are you seated? I hope you have a table."

"Sure. This way…"

***

"*He fills me up….!*" Rachel belts out to an adoring audience. She's getting the right notes, though she's struggling with her pitch and volume. But more than the music and how she's singing, she's thinking about the lyrics. Somehow, Doug doesn't quite measure up against Whitney's standard. But she won't worry about that. Besides, is there any man than can measure up?

Funnily enough, Doug stands and gives her an ovation for her performance, thinking she meant the song as a devotion to him. He gives her a hug and a kiss when she comes down from the stage, to the applause of the audience. She doesn't try to correct his impression, but smiles and giggles when her friends tell her how great she sounded. Her confidence is raised.

She finds herself looking continually in the corner where Ejike is seated, obviously engrossed in his date. She's not jealous. Why should she be? But it seems strange that neither of them has gone to greet the other. Maybe she should go over there… *No, I won't.*

"So, Rachel… How are wedding plans coming along?" Bose asks, jolting her friend back to Earth. Wow, she is getting married in just four months!

***

"Hey, babe. You having a good time?" Doug leans into Rachel to ask.

She smiles and nods. Honestly, she is having fun. It may not be as romantic as some other settings, but she is happy that she's out with Doug and her friends. She and Doug always have fun when they go out together.

He takes her hand and locks it with his, looking at her with passion in his eyes. "You're special, you know?" he says. Sometimes, he can be so sweet. "I can't believe how lucky I am that you're here with me. Thank you."

At times like this, she really believes he loves her. She just has to stop overthinking this, and she'll soon fall head over heels for him too. She can definitely feel a tug in her heart as she looks into his face. "Thank you too…"

He grins and kisses her softly on her lips. The Karaoke screen announces the next song. Doug whispers, and she manages to hear, "This is for you, babe."

Rachel feels butterflies in her tummy. She knows the song, and it's one of her favourites. And as Doug sings the lyrics to Jagged Edge's "I Gotta Be", she knows that the song was carefully chosen. She remembers her radio chat with Kenneth today, and shakes her head, smiling. *It's the thought that counts.*

She happily gives him a standing ovation when he's done singing. When he alights the stage, he takes her in his arms and says with deep emotion, "I gotta be the one you love…because I love you so much."

And she hears herself saying, "I love you too…" Well, if

it's not about the feelings, then it's the truth.

They sway side to side in rhythm to Wyclef's and Lauren Hill's duet, "Turn Your Lights Down Low", which now plays through the speakers. They are joined by a few other couples who also love the song. As they dance snug together, their tongues tango in a lovers' kiss. Now, this feels like Valentine's Day.

When her second song comes up, Rachel's ready and excited to take the stage. She's not bothered about the lyrics this time. It's all about the way the music makes her feel on top of the world. And she sings with flair and dances with freedom.

CHAPTER FIFTEEN

The days are moving fast, and there's still so much to be done ahead of the wedding. The invitations are yet to be sent out, though the designs have now been approved. The wedding planner is hard at work coordinating all the vendors, and Rachel has had a couple of meetings with her, Mrs Eden, and Rochelle too, to agree on the decorations, cake, menu list, and other special logistical considerations for the day. So far, Doug has made little input into the wedding ceremonies, particularly the reception, which is the biggest and most costly portion of the whole wedding. Rachel has decided to leave him with the responsibility of choosing the band, so that he feels more involved.

The day for the marriage introduction ceremony soon comes. The house is abuzz with so many new faces and voices. The Olumides and the Folushos are both represented, though the father of the groom remains AWOL. On the bride's side, few of her mother's relatives are able to make the occasion, while lots of her father's relatives are on ground to make sure proper traditional protocols are followed.

Rachel is both excited and nervous about the introduction. Things have been going really well between her and Doug.

They've continued their marriage counselling sessions with one of the pastors of her church, where the white wedding ceremony is to be held. After the introduction, they are also supposed to go to the marriage registry to announce their intent to marry with a public notice. It's all beginning to feel too real.

This is really happening…to me, Rachel thinks to herself, as she gets dressed for the introduction ceremony. Rochelle is in Rachel's room, assisting her, while Mrs Eden is with the elders downstairs. Doug is already downstairs with the elders, and she's just waiting to be called down so that he can confirm that she is the one he has chosen to be his wife.

Before long, Aunty Joy comes and calls them to come downstairs. It's time for the bride to be chosen. Rachel and Rochelle strike one last pose for the camera.

***

"Can I have the key to your car, please?"

Rachel turns to look at Doug. The ceremony is over, but a number of his relatives are still hanging around. He's looking at her expectantly, his hand out to collect the key. "What car?"

"The Mazda, of course."

"Why?"

"I need to drop my mom and siblings at the airport."

"But you have the Toyota!"

"I told Nike he could use it. He's dropping off some of our relatives too."

"Huh?! You told Nike he could drive my car…without asking me?!"

"Please can you not make a scene now…? He's a good driver, and I'll collect the car from him when I get home tonight…"

"How?! With the Mazda? What car am I supposed to use?"

"Stop being dramatic, Rachel. You have so many cars in

this house and drivers too. If you need to go anywhere, you're sorted. You can always use Uber too…"

Rachel is stupefied. "And you can't, *because*…?"

"Don't make me beg, nau. Rache. I promised them a lift. I don't want them to take Uber. Can you just give me the key?" Doug demands.

Reluctantly, Rachel hands over the key to her precious Mazda. Everyone has been watching her argue with Doug about using her car, and she is starting to feel petty. She struggles to smile as she bids safe journey to his family, who bundle into her car to be driven to the local airport.

She goes up to her room and tries not to slam the door in her frustration. Why is she so angry? It's not a big deal. It's just a car. *No! It's the way he asked. The way he committed himself without asking me. It was so presumptuous and controlling!*

There's a knock at the door. Rachel doesn't want to be bothered, but answers, "Come in…"

Rochelle opens the door. "Hey, we're going for a barbecue. You want to come?"

Rachel looks at her sister. She wants to say "no", because she doesn't really feel in the mood. But Rochelle rarely invites her out. "Ummm… Okay. Thanks."

"Where's Doug?" she asks.

"He went to drop off his family."

"Oh, okay. We're going now. You ready?"

"Yes… Just give me a minute to change."

"Where's your car?" Rochelle asks, when they get outside.

"Doug took it."

"Both cars?!"

"Yes," she answers solemnly.

"Hmmm… Okay. I guess you're riding with us."

***

They drive into an estate in Lekki. The multitude of cars parked on the street near a house buzzing with loud music confirm that they have arrived at their destination. Rachel follows Rochelle and Ekene as they walk into the house, greeting a few of their friends along the way.

"Hey, you guys! Glad you could make it," Ejike greets his sister-in-law and brother. They both hug him before presenting him with gifts. Rachel just stares at Ejike, surprised that he would be the owner of the home and the reason for the celebration. Why hadn't anyone told her?

"Hey, Rache," he greets her warmly. "Thanks for coming."

"Ummm... I didn't know this was your thing..."

"Otherwise, you wouldn't have come?"

She's shocked by his response. "Of course not! Why would you say that?"

Ejike shrugs. "I told them not to tell you. I know it's your introduction today, so you might have had other plans for tonight."

Rachel lets out a deep breath, wondering about the emotions that seem to be making it harder for her to breathe. She gasps as she looks about, seeking to conceal her discomfort.

"Where's Doug?" Ejike asks.

"He took his family to the airport."

"Oh, okay. Well, I'm glad you came."

Rachel nods, not knowing what else to do. She looks about for Ekene and Rochelle and sees that they've already settled down with some chops from the grill. She heads towards them in an effort to stay away from Ejike.

"Why didn't you tell me we were coming here?!" she demands to know.

"Is there a problem? Don't you like Ejike?" Rochelle asks.

Rachel blushes at the question. "Of course, I do. I just don't know why it was a secret."

"He was just being considerate of you and Doug, Rache," Ekene answers.

Hmmm... She lets out a sigh. "So, what... Is it his

birthday or something?"

Ekene nods. "Yup. That, and he's completed his PhD."

"Oh, wow," she smiles. "That's great news."

***

Rachel eventually decides to get herself some chops at the grill. Ejike is engrossed in conversation with a couple of his friends at the other end of the room, so her chances of bumping into him are slim. The options are too many. She eventually settles for the lamb chops and a burger.

"I'll have the same…"

The hairs on her neck stand to attention at the raspy masculine voice beside her. She turns to see Ejike smiling cheekily at her. She can't help but smile too. Something in her chest feels hot. In a good way. But she steps back from the grill, in case it's the cause.

"So, how are you, Rache?" Ejike asks, his eyes searching hers.

"I'm fine," she breathes. "I hear congratulations are in order."

He beams. "Yes, thanks!"

"And Happy Birthday too…"

"Thank you, Rachel."

Their burgers are ready and they collect them from the grill attendant.

"Come… Let's sit by the pond."

"You have a pond?!"

"Yes, I do. It's the only way I can keep pets."

"What, you're allergic?"

"Nah… Just not an animal person. Too much work looking after dogs and cats."

"Hmmm… Are you just a *scaredy*-cat?" Rachel teases.

"Yup. Scared shitless!" he laughs, and she joins in.

"Me too!"

They enjoy momentary silence in the short walk to the pond hidden behind shrubs in his backyard. There are three stone stools around it, and they take one each to sit on. Rachel looks back at the party they've separated themselves from. The music is still very loud, but at least they can hold a decent conversation.

"So, how's Doug?"

Rachel takes in a deep breath and answers, "He's fine."

Ejike nods.

"How's your girlfriend?"

"*My girlfriend?*"

Rachel looks at him, a little surprised. Are there that many?! "I thought you were on a date on Valentine's Day…?"

"Oh… Tonye. She's fine. We're just friends."

Hmmm… "You didn't look like 'just friends'…"

Ejike looks up at Rachel, thinking she sounded a little jealous. "Well, she's an ex. And for a while, I thought we could give it another try… But…"

Rachel raises a brow. "But…?"

"I wasn't ready," Ejike says, looking down at his plate. "And she isn't the one." *Because I'm in love with someone else…*

"Oh, I'm sorry."

He shrugs. "I'm not. I think when it comes to marriage, it's better to be sure. I need to be with someone who makes me feel alive…you know? Someone with whom I appreciate every breath…"

Rachel nods and suddenly feels breathless. She turns her attention to her plate. The heat in her chest now burns. She shouldn't be here with Ejike. "I think we should get back to your party. Your other guests will be missing you."

"I doubt it…" he says but stands up with her. Reluctantly, he follows her back to the crowd and watches as she enters the guest bathroom when they're back inside the house.

***

"So, is Doug coming to get you?" Rochelle asks Rachel, who's bowed over her mobile phone.

"No, I don't think so. I haven't been able to reach him. I guess I'll take an Uber."

"Why? Ejike can drop you at home," Ekene says.

Rachel looks up, slightly alarmed. "No… I'll be fine. Besides, he can't leave his party…"

"Sure, I can," Ejike affirms, coming to sit on the arm of Rachel's chair. "The party is a wrap anyway. Just give me like 20 minutes, and we'll go."

Rachel looks between Rochelle and Ekene. "Uber will be easier. He doesn't need to."

"It's late. You should let him drop you, Rache. We're off now," Ekene stands up and supports his pregnant wife to her feet.

"Okay. Bye…" she says after them. She heaves a sigh.

A few minutes later, the music goes off, and the house begins to empty. Rachel watches as Ejike thanks and sends off his friends one by one. She looks at her watch, 9:10pm. It's really not that late, she thinks.

"Alright… Let me take you home," Ejike says, as he leads the way out of the house to his car.

Rachel recognises the blue Hyundai Doug used to drive. The number plate even looks the same. She withholds her comment until they enter the car, and she looks about. The interior is the same.

"Isn't this Doug's car?"

"What makes you say that?"

"It looks exactly like it… And the plate number too."

"No, it's my car. I lent it to Doug while I was in Port Harcourt."

"Oh…" Rachel says, thinking Doug never gave the impression that he wasn't the owner of the car.

"No problem, I hope…"

"It's just… He said it was recalled by the manufacturer."

Ejike chuckles. "No… Just by the owner."

Rachel swallows as Ejike pulls out of the driveway and

unto the street. Why would Doug lie to her about something so simple? What else could he have lied about; she worries as they drive in silence.

"I hope you had a good night, Rache," Ejike says, as he drives into her parents' compound.

She turns to him and smiles. "Thanks. I did. And thanks for the lift home."

"It was my pleasure."

Awkwardly, she opens the car door and alights the car. It's then she notices her Mazda in her parking space, and Doug walking towards her. She feels incredible relief at seeing her car and a little apprehension at seeing Doug.

"What's going on?" he asks when he reaches Ejike's car.

"I just thought I should give her a lift home…"

"From???"

"I was at his birthday party with Rochelle and Ekene. I sent you messages."

"Birthday? My bad, I forgot. You should have reminded me, Ejike."

Ejike shrugs. "You had other things going on."

"Yeah…" Doug takes Rachel in his arms and kisses her on her lips. He turns back to Ejike. "I owe you one." He puts his arm around Rachel's shoulder and turns her towards the mansion, away from Ejike.

Rachel feels like she's being pulled off and takes a hold of Doug's arm to release herself from his hold. Turning back around, still holding Doug's hand – or he's holding hers – she waves 'bye' to Ejike.

"Thanks again, Ejike."

"You're welcome, Rache," he replies, before getting back in his car and reversing out.

Lord, I feel so helpless! She's going to marry this man, and there's nothing I can do about it. Why do I feel this way for her? I don't want to feel this way anymore. Please, tell me what to do…

CHAPTER SIXTEEN

"So, what was that about?" Doug asks when they get in the privacy of Rachel's room.

The apprehension has returned. Rachel puts her purse down on her dressing table and turns to look at Doug. "What's what about?"

"That?!" Doug raises his voice, his finger pointing in the direction they came. "What were you doing in his car?!"

"Are you *serious* right now?!"

"Do I look like I'm joking?!"

"You took my car! Both my cars! And you didn't respond to any of my messages. And besides, he's my brother-in-law. What's your problem?!"

"I don't like the way he looks at you. I don't trust him, Rachel. He's bad news, and I need you to keep your distance from him."

"What?! I thought you guys were friends…"

Doug exhales dramatically. "It's a long story, Rache. But for Ejike, it's always about winning. He thinks he can get any woman to fall for him, and no woman is safe from his advances. I know he seems like a good guy, but…looks can be deceiving."

Rachel nods, feeling like she knew that already. "Fine. I'll keep my distance." She swallows.

Doug lets out a sigh and goes to hold her. "Thanks, Rachel. Your trust in me means so much." He raises her chin up to look at her. "I'm sorry I left you alone today. I should have just called Uber for them, but… I guess I wanted to impress them."

Rachel swallows and nods. She moves out of his arms, thinking about the Hyundai, wondering if she should say something. "Why did you lie to me?"

"What are you talking about?"

"You told me your car had a fault and was recalled by the manufacturer…"

"Oh, that…" He takes a deep breath. "What did Ejike tell you?"

"Does it matter?! I only want the truth." Rachel looks at Doug, not quite sure what reaction she's expecting.

He takes her hand and pulls her to sit down on the bed. "I'm sorry I lied about that."

"Why?" she looks at him, baffled.

"Look, it was just an honest mistake. You thought it was my car. I didn't want to correct you."

"So, it's *my* fault now?"

"Why are you being like this, Rache? I said I'm sorry. You have to understand that being with someone like you would be daunting for a man like me. I just didn't want you to see me any less worthy…"

"So, you pretended to be something you are not…?" Rachel stands up, angry. "If you can lie about that, what else are you lying about?"

"Now, you're blowing things out of proportion, Rachel. I've been honest with you about who I am. You know that. Please, don't make this an issue."

"I think you need to go."

"What?!"

"Doug, I just need some space to think things through.

I'm starting to feel like I don't know you."

Doug shakes his head. "You know this is *horse shit*, right?! I know it's Ejike that's poisoned you against me. You need to be careful who you're listening to, Rachel."

She nods. "I've heard you. Please go."

Doug fumes and marches to the door. He doesn't say "Bye". He doesn't say anything. She hears the front door of her home slam shut. And she's shocked to hear her Mazda car horn, and the gates open moments later. *Is he really driving off with my car???! How dare he?!!!*

***

God, what kind of man is this? Why would he behave this way…? Am I really doing the right thing, marrying him? Lord, please, I need Your guidance…

Rachel prays intermittently, as she struggles to understand her relationship with Doug. Her heart is filled with so much anguish and anxiety. She's also feeling rage at his nerve last night. After depriving her of her car all day, he didn't hesitate to take it home with him, even after their fight. As if he wasn't even listening to her!

She has to go to church this morning, but she doesn't have a car, so she has to call an Uber. How annoying! She books the ride and then hears the horn of her Mazda 3 outside. *Oh, thank God, he brought it back.* Behind him, Nike drives the Toyota into the compound.

Rachel hurries downstairs to meet them. When she gets outside, she sticks out her hand for her Mazda key, her other hand on her hips, and Doug gives it to her. She's too angry to say a word. She wants to ask him for the key to the Toyota too, but hopes he would spare them the embarrassment and just hand it over. But he only walks past her, into her home.

Nike steps out of the Toyota. "Good morning, Rachel. How are you?"

She has to adjust her mood for him. She forces a smile.

"Good morning."

She enters the house in search of Doug. She hears the guest toilet flush and, moments later, he comes out. And out the front door he goes again, without saying a word to her. Doesn't he realise what he has done?!

She follows him outside. Angry, she asks, "Can I have the Toyota key, please?"

He stops and turns to her, obviously angry too. "Why?"

"Because it's my car, and I want the key!"

"I'm using it," he says, turning around to enter the driver's seat.

"Doug!"

"No need to be nasty, Rache. We'll talk about it later..." he says, before getting behind the wheel and shutting the door.

Nike looks uncomfortable, but enters the passenger seat. Rachel watches as the gate opens again, and Doug drives out with her car. *No, I can't marry this man!*

***

A whole day goes by, and Rachel doesn't hear from Doug. She's so hurt, upset and angry. How had she not seen this before?

She's supposed to meet with the wedding planner today, and gets a call from her to confirm their meeting time. They have three months until this wedding. She can still put a stop to it.

"The wedding is off!" she says to the planner.

"Rachel, are you okay?"

"The wedding is off. We broke up."

"Okay... Well, please talk your mom or something. We can't cancel anything until your parents confirm that it's officially called off. I hope you guys work it out."

Rachel doesn't know what to say. She just hangs up the call. How will she tell her step-mom that she doesn't want to marry Doug anymore? Will she even understand?

When her father returns from work that evening, she gets the courage to go up to their quarters and tell them about the change in her relationship with Doug. When she gets in their room, she realises how afraid she is of disappointing them. They've spent so much on this venture already. And at this point, the invitations have been sent out. Their reputation is also at stake…

"I can't marry Doug," she manages to say through trembles.

Husband and wife look at each other, and then at Rachel. Mrs Eden takes the cue and the responsibility for damage control. She stands up and goes to give Rachel a hug. Rachel breaks down in tears and follows her mother as she leads her to her suite.

"Let's talk," she says.

***

Mrs Eden listens as Rachel recounts the incidents of the last 72 hours, and how she feels like she doesn't know Doug anymore.

"I know we've spent so much already…and I feel bad, but I can't go through with the wedding…" Rachel cries.

"It's okay, Rachel. It's really not about the money. It's about your happiness."

Rachel looks up at her step-mom, surprised that she'd feel that way. She nods and smiles and listens as Mrs Eden continues.

"You see, men are like babies. We think they grow up and mature because they become big, but they remain babies. Like babies, they are very needy for validation from their women. They need the assurance that you believe in them, and you support them. And as they grow, it gets worse, because apart from needing your support, they need to be *needed* by you. All men! Every one of them. Even your father."

Rachel swallows.

"What Doug did isn't really that unusual. I know it hurts. It's annoying. But he's just trying to see how much you love him. And his case may be worse because he might feel insecure about your background, so there's a greater need to prove himself. But you can't hold it against him. As long as you believe in who he is, and who he can become, you just have to show him your unconditional support. He needs to know that he is safe with you and, if he feels safe, he will love you so much. When he has his own money, he will just spoil you finish!" Mrs Eden laughs.

Rachel can't help but laugh. It all rings true to her.

"You see your dad; what was he when we were dating? He was not the big man that he is today. Even okada bike, we would ride it together! It doesn't mean anything. But because I was there when he was down, *lai lai, nobody* can take him from me now! You just have to know what you want, see it, and fight for it. You are the one who will build Doug. If you want the one that is already made...*hmmm*... Be careful, because that one can use you like toilet paper!"

Rachel sighs, thinking of Ejike. Yeah, she has been warned many times about him.

"Look, Rachel. In marriage, there are many offences, but it is only love and forgiveness that will make it last. And you need to start showing that you are the kind that will last, by showing him love and forgiveness now. I beg you, because I don't want you to be a lonely spinster, just try and forgive him, and work on your issues. Me too, I can talk to him for you. Just to be sure he also appreciates how precious you are."

Rachel nods. "Thank you. I appreciate it."

Mrs Eden extends her hand to wipe Rachel's teary face. "It is okay. No more crying, eh? These things happen. You are a bride, and you too will dance your own dance soon. Cheer up!"

"Thank you, mom!" Rachel says, as she goes in for another

hug. She really needed this guidance.

***

The following evening, Rachel's in her room, browsing social media on her phone, when she hears a knock on the door. "Come in," she answers, lazily.

She's surprised to see Doug step into her room looking sheepish. It's now been over 48 hours since she last heard from him, and she's been struggling with forgiving him, especially as he's shown no remorse for anything he's done. She swallows, looking at him, remembering her talk with her step-mom.

"Hi, Rachel," he says, gently, walking into her room and shutting the door behind him.

She's now wondering if he has had that talk with Mrs Eden. She hadn't heard his (her) car horn, so she doesn't have a clue how long he's been in her home. At least he's looking sober. Apologetic. But is that amusement??!

"What do you want?" she hears herself say. She's still angry. He has to try a little!

"I'm sorry, Rachel," he says, sitting on the edge of her bed, looking at her. "I'm really, very sorry."

She swallows. Okay, that's better. *Go on...*

"I acted like a fool. I was just scared… I thought you would reject me, and I just wanted to act as if it wouldn't affect me. But I was stupid, and I hurt you. I'm so sorry."

She looks into his face, and he's sincere. Her anger melts away. She reaches out to him and hugs him. "I'm sorry too."

Maybe she did blow things out of proportion and act like a brat over her cars. She should have been thinking about his family's comfort too and even offered her cars or maybe even organised transport for them. She really needs to make more effort to show him that she is his right-hand woman, and not just a rich girl with a pretty face.

"I want you to feel safe with me, Doug. I'm sorry if I made you feel unwanted. I love you."

"And I love you, Rache! I love you so much."

And he leans into her and kisses her passionately. They lie down together on the bed and continue to kiss and cuddle, both ecstatic that they are still going to get married after all.

CHAPTER SEVENTEEN

"So, how did you get on with the exercises I gave you last week?" the counsellor asks at their weekly session. With just over a month to their wedding, they are in their final sessions of the counselling programme.

Doug and Rachel both nod. "It was good," Rachel says.

"So, can I see your financial plan for the first year of your marriage?"

Doug brings out a sheet he and Rachel had worked on earlier in the day. It tends to be the case that they forget to do their assignments until the day of their counselling session. He presents it to the counsellor, who goes through it like it is an exam paper.

"So, is this based on your current *real* income?" the counsellor asks, an eye-brow raised at the couple before him.

Doug shifts in his seat. "I guess we were a bit optimistic. I'm expecting a few jobs to fall into place."

"Okay… It's not bad. At least, this should have got you thinking about the sort of expenses you would have living together and your financial responsibility to each other."

They both nod.

"Alright. At this stage, you should know a lot more about each other; your personality traits, personal preferences, habits, desires, goals and more. You should be able to develop a character profile for each other, which shows true knowledge and appreciation for the person you are about to be joined with in marriage." The counsellor hands them three new sheets each. "Go through these and let's start work on your character profiles."

Rachel studies the sheets before her. She's able to answer positively for a lot of the questions about Doug. Does he get easily angry? *No.* Does he usually demand his own way? *No.* Does he usually say what he means? *Hmmm...* Does he usually do what he says? *Hmmm...*

He doesn't score very well in the trust department. She'd identified this before, when they had done their "Can't Stands" and "Must-Haves". Trust for her was a must-have and dishonesty, a can't stand. With the incident of their big fight fresh on her mind at the time, she'd considered that a red flag. Since, she'd been able to observe him and identified more instances when he conveniently chose to bend the truth.

"So, what are the character flaws you have identified so far?" the counsellor directs.

Doug looks at Rachel and smiles. He shakes his head and replies. "Rachel has a really strong character... The only thing is perhaps her emotional maturity. I'm sorry, babe, but you can be very easily riled up about small things."

Hmmm... Rachel's thinking about what Doug's calling small things. They tend to be things they disagree on, based on her moral compass. To her, they are not small issues.

"Ummm.... I think Doug is pretty easy going, but I think it's sometimes a bad thing when he behaves irresponsibly. I also have an issue with how freely he is able to lie. He sometimes comes across as a dishonest person."

"Hmmm... Do you have any examples of these occasions of dishonesty?" the counsellor asks.

"Well, it's not often big lies. Like, he will be in the

bathroom, and someone is waiting to meet him somewhere. He will just say he's on the way and is stuck in traffic. I think such lies are really unnecessary."

The counsellor smiles and looks at Doug, who's looking rather amused. "Anything else?"

"It's just stuff like that generally. I just feel like, as Christians, we should be truthful people whose words are trustworthy."

To her surprise, the counsellor chuckles, before he responds. "Ideally, we should always tell the truth, but your expectation of trustworthiness may be too high. This is Nigeria, and you can probably think of many instances when *you* have withheld the truth or even padded it, to get out of a shady situation. I mean, you both come from different backgrounds and, I may be wrong but, I think what you're identifying is a street-wise survival trait, that isn't really about Doug's character as a Christian."

Hmmm…

"Thank you, Sir. I try to get her to see it sometimes. You can't just be truthful to everyone all the time. Even something like telling your girlfriend she has a good voice, when she really can't sing… It's just being diplomatic. For me, it's all about emotional intelligence," Doug says. *Ouch! Was that a dig at my singing ability???*

The counsellor nods, and Rachel looks between the two of them. Apparently, her expectations of truthfulness and trustworthiness are too high…

"Were there other things you found concerning…?" the counsellor asks, moving on.

Rachel shakes her head, still processing how the last subject was resolved.

***

It's her day off work, and Rachel is at home planning the baby shower for her sister. She had invited a few of Rochelle's friends to the house to agree on the theme, venue and budget for the shower. Everyone seems to think a shower at the Eden mansion makes the most sense and would be the most cost-effective.

They are just wrapping up on plans, when the steward approaches Rachel, saying that there's a man in the waiting room requesting to see her. Rachel excuses herself, trying to ignore the whispers of the other ladies, who know that she's just a month away from getting married.

She opens the door to the waiting area and is surprised to see Ejike sitting there. Why would they have presented him as a stranger, she wonders?

"Hey, Ejike… Why didn't you just come in?"

"I noticed you were busy… I didn't want to interrupt." He stands up. "How are you, Rachel?"

She smiles and nods. "I'm good. What brings you here?"

"I need to talk to you about something… I'd really rather it's private."

"Oh, okay. Should I just finish up first?"

"Please. No rush," Ejike smiles.

"Okay, then. I'll probably be another ten minutes."

He nods and she turns back around to her friends. He sits down and swallows, gathering his nerve. It's now or never.

***

After the ladies leave, a few ogling the handsome man in the waiting room on their way out, Rachel invites Ejike into the lounge.

"I think the lounge is rather open," he says.

"Oh, right. You wanted privacy. You want to go outside or something?"

"Here seems fine," he says, indicating the room he'd been waiting in.

"Okay, sure." Rachel takes a seat and then considers if he might be thirsty or hungry. "Can I get you something…?"

"I'm fine, Rachel. I promise."

She nods and smiles. She's starting to feel a little nervous.

What could he want to talk to her about?

"Rachel…" he breathes out. "I have been a fool." She raises a brow. "I was afraid and unsure, and I didn't let you know how much you mean to me…"

She's looking confused. "I don't understand."

"I'm in love with you, Rachel."

Silence.

"I have been for a very long time. I didn't know how to tell you. I thought things would naturally end between you and Doug, and I'd get my chance… I missed so many opportunities. But I feel you need to know this, before you marry him. *I love you.*"

"But…you don't even know me…"

"I do. I really do. I've been watching you. I've been listening to your radio shows. You give such good advice! Sometimes, I want to call in and just encourage you. We've spoken a few times, and I know you are the same woman I hear on the radio, only more glorious in person…"

Wow… Almost sounds like idolatry, Rachel thinks. She is pleased to know that he's been listening to her shows, though. Doug seems to have dropped the ball on that, she thinks.

"Okay. So, you know me. But I'm getting married. To your *friend*…"

"You're not married yet. And Doug and I haven't really been friends in months… If I'm honest, years actually. And that…the idea of that we were friends, prevented me from coming after you. He is not the one for you, Rachel. I'm sorry I'm saying this now, but you can't marry him!"

Rachel is shaking. *The nerve of him!* "How can you come here and say that to me…a month before my wedding day?! Are you so selfish?!"

"I'm sorry…"

"Are you proposing marriage? Are you ready to marry me?!"

"I just thought, we could give it a try and…"

Rachel is laughing. "Are you kidding me? Give it a *try*?! I'm 32 years old. I don't have time for time-wasters. You say you love me, that *you're in love* with me, and you don't want me to marry Doug, but you don't want to marry me either!"

Ejike gets on his knees and holds her hand. "I do, I do. I just thought it's not something we would rush into. But at least, if you're not with Doug, we can be together. I know I'm late, Rachel, but I'm not too late. *Please…*"

Rachel puts her other hand on her head, massaging away a growing headache. Why is this happening? Why now? She is finally in a good state of mind, committed to the idea of her and Doug forever… Is this the devil's temptation? Some kind of sabotage?!

"Say something, Rachel…"

"Please sit down." He does. She's looking into his eyes. "I really wish you had said something before, Ejike. I honestly like you, despite my efforts not to. But I don't feel I can trust you now. I don't feel safe with you… I don't feel like I know you enough. I also made a commitment to Doug that I want to honour. At least, unless God shows me otherwise. I'm sorry, this is bigger than you and me."

The tears run freely from Ejike's eyes as he realises that he has failed. He is indeed too late. She's gone. At this point, nothing he says about Doug would change her mind. She'd only see it as a jealous attack on his character. He sobs.

Rachel watches him for a moment, not knowing what to do. She can't hear her heart. She can't hear her spirit. Her mind is the only vocal part, and it's telling her that she made the right decision. She's shown herself to be loyal.

"I think you need to go," she says at last, standing up to leave the room.

Ejike nods, still crying, unable to believe his loss. How could this happen?!

***

Some days later, Doug and Rachel are out taking their premarital photos, ahead of the big day. They have set apart the whole day to do things together, with a photographer following them and recording their interactions. It's a romantic day indeed, with a stroll in the park, a boat ride along the Lagos Lagoon, a visit to an Arts Gallery and finally, a dinner at a four-star hotel.

The couple have never been so happy and in sync. Everything about the day is perfect. The weather is just right, with the sun shining bright. The wind is strong, blowing Rachel's weavon wildly as they sail. The roads are free, minimising their stress to get to various locations, and the food is exquisite.

They made a stopover at the Eden mansion to change into their dinner wear, but before then, they took pictures in their casual wear around the stylishly furnished home. After they changed, they took more pictures in their dinner attire, before heading over to the hotel.

Doug is dressed in a new, red shirt and jeans, looking fresh, and Rachel is dressed in a short, mustard, slim-fitting, jersey dress, looking cute and sexy. They can't seem to keep their eyes (and hands) off each other, as they smile often and laugh a lot.

"Today was perfect," Rachel says over dinner.

"Absolutely!"

"So, are you ready?"

"For?"

"The big day. Have your groomsmen sewn their suits? Have you got everything for the trad wedding? Do you need help with anything?"

Doug shrugs. "We're pretty ready… But, can we not talk about that right now?"

"Sure," she smiles. "What do you want to talk about?"

"How beautiful you are…" Rachel blushes. "How you make me feel like the luckiest man alive. How I can't wait to finally make love to you..."

Rachel throws her head back and laughs out loud. "Hmmm... *That...*"

"Yes, all of that. And our kids too... How I'm looking forward to being a daddy, and having a little me and a little you running around."

She smiles. "I'm looking forward to all those things too..."

"Yeah, baby!" he says, indicating, with two fingers, for her to lean over for a kiss.

The photographer captures the picture-perfect shot.

CHAPTER EIGHTEEN

The following weekend, the girls are together again, this time, all dressed ready to celebrate their sister and friend. The main lounge in the Eden mansion has been decorated for purpose, with blue and pink balloons and ribbons. Next to the organiser's board is a confectionary and dessert table, where a lovely, two tier, white cake sits, with blue and pink icing lining the circumference. And on the other side of the room is the table for gifts, which is considerably stocked.

They all sit in anticipation of the arrival of the special guest, who isn't due for another five minutes. When they hear the horn of her car outside, indicating her arrival, they scramble for a place to hide from which they will shout "SURPRISE!!!" when the door to the lounge opens. However, there seems to be some delay in this inevitable occurrence, and some ladies are tired of their squatting positions. About to arise, the door swings open, and in waddles a heavily pregnant Rochelle!

"SURPRISE!!!" they shout at last in unison.

Her joyful laughter fills the air as she beholds her friends. She's indeed surprised, as her husband had told her that her mother had requested to speak to them about something. She happily waddles further into the room, being heavy at seven and a half months pregnant. She hugs her friends and her sister, who have organised such a special event for her.

"Thanks, guys!" she says when she finally settles into her ceremonial seat, a special settee reserved for her in a corner of the room.

"What took you so long...? We heard your car and all got into place," Rachel asks.

"I had to pee!" Rochelle giggles. "And this baby is heavy!"

The ladies join in giggles.

***

Rachel's happy about the success of Rochelle's shower. A sizable amount of her friends were able to make it, and most brought gifts, which was nice. They also played lots of games that got her more excited about the fact that she would be getting married shortly, and would soon be expecting her own children.

"How did it go today?" Doug asks later that evening when they see.

"It was great. Rochelle had lots of fun. The cake was really nice too!"

"Any left?"

"Yeah... Let me go cut you a slice," Rachel beams at Doug.

"Just a little! I have to fit into my suit in three weeks." They both laugh, and she leaves for the kitchen to bring some cake for her fiancé.

"You're right! That was delicious," Doug says when he's devoured his piece.

"Yeah... They are the same people that are baking our wedding cake. Their cakes are really out of this world."

"Hmmm..." Doug moans. He pulls Rachel closer to him, where he's lying on the bed. "Do you know what else is out of this world?"

She giggles in anticipation. "What?"

"Kissing you!" She beams as he does so. "You have the

softest, sweetest lips…"

"And you're a really good kisser!" she joins in their tease.

"I'm only good because I'm kissing you," he returns smoothly.

She laughs. "What drug are you on?" He nibbles her lips sensually, his hands stepping out of line.

"It's the love drug, baby!"

She shakes her head at him and releases herself. "Let's take it easy, abeg. Maybe we can work on our assignment for a change."

"Hmmm…" he grunts, leaning back and folding his hands behind his head. "Okay."

She rewards him with a quick kiss, before going to get her homework sheet from this week's counselling session.

***

The next day, after attending church together, something they've been doing since they reconciled two months ago, Doug decides to stop over at the Palms Shopping Mall, Lekki. He is in need of a tie and a few other things. They walk through the mall in each other's arms, annoying the singles trying to pass by quickly and having to dodge them.

Before leaving, Doug offers to get Rachel some ice cream, and she's never been able to turn down an offer of ice cream. They order one of the signature cones by Coldstone Creamery and settle in the food court to enjoy their treat. Rachel's happy to be treated by Doug. It doesn't happen often, because he's not a big spender, but it's always nice when it does.

They are both hungry, and Doug suggests that they return to her home to eat instead of eating out. There's usually food prepared at home, so it sounds like a good idea. They return with their light shopping to her Mazda car, in the parking lot. Doug gets behind the wheel and drives them to her home.

Rachel leads the way into the house and is surprised by her own friends and sister, as she opens the door into the main lounge.

"CONGRATULATIONS!!!" they shout in unison.

Rachel giggles and turns to give Doug a friendly nudge. So, he'd just been delaying her at the mall. He looks up from his phone, where he'd kept himself engrossed, and beams back at her.

"Oh, wow! I'm really surprised. Thanks, everyone!" Rachel says, admiring the decoration of her home with colourful ribbons, balloons, and bridal shower banners.

"Please, where's the food?" Doug asks, with mirth. Rochelle points to the dining area. Rachel giggles, thinking she'd like to start with that too.

The dining table is set for 12, and Rachel is shown to her seat at the top of the banquet. There, she's crowned the bride and draped in a pink, bridal sash. Doug makes himself scarce in her bedroom, after collecting his plate of food from the kitchen.

Rachel is happy to see so many of her girlfriends that she hasn't seen in a while. She's excited about the games and activities they'll get up to afterwards, but the lunch is really the highlight of the celebration.

***

As their wedding day draws nearer, Rachel and Doug begin to post their premarital pictures on social media. The goodwill messages are pouring in from everywhere. They are a gorgeous couple, is the general sentiment. Rachel's all the more excited. She can't wait to wear her beautiful, white gown and walk down the aisle to her destiny.

"*Beautiful picture!*" Ekene writes in response to the new display picture Rachel has put on her WhatsApp, of her and Doug on a boat, her hair flying in the wind.

"*Thank you* 😁" she replies.

"*You must be very excited.*"

"*I am* 🙂 *How's Rochelle?*"

"She's good! We're flying to the US the day after your wedding. You know we're close to our delivery date."

"I know!!! She better keep it together until then. I can't have her water breaking in the middle of my ceremony!"

"Lol! No, we can't."

Rachel beams. She wants to ask about Ejike. They haven't spoken since his visit to her home last month.

"How's Ejike?"

"He's fine. He's actually moving to the States this month. He got a job offer!"

"You're kidding. Congrats to him! When's he going?"

"He should be there before us."

"You mean, he's not coming for my wedding?!"

"No, he's not. He's still around, though… In case you want to talk to him."

"Oh, okay."

"Later, Rachel!"

"Yeah… Later."

So, Ejike is leaving… Does she want to talk to him? What would she say? It's better she leaves it alone. If he wants to say 'bye', he would.

***

Before long, it's the day of the traditional wedding. The Eden mansion is abuzz again. Chief Eden is very happy, indeed. One of his daughters is carrying his first grandchild, and the other is about to get married, and will soon have her own family. His first son has also announced his engagement to his long-time girlfriend, who they will be meeting for the first time on Rachel's white wedding day. He is a blessed man.

The bride is looking breath-taking in her traditional attire. The coral beads set in gold, that adorn her neck and hands, enhance the burgundy and gold wrap she's tying. Her hair and make-up are exceptional, making her look like the queen she is. Chief Eden beholds his daughter with affection and joy, as she poses for the cameras.

"Come, let us take our photo," he says to her, and she beams at him.

After a few shots, Richard joins them, and Ryan too. The brothers later take their personal photos with their sister and tell her how gorgeous she looks. Rochelle is taking it easy downstairs, being heavily pregnant. She beams when she spots her sister coming down the stairs. "Beautiful!" she mouths.

Rachel is aglow. Her special day has come. Today, she is a bride, tomorrow, she'll be a wife. God has made it all possible.

***

The mother of the bride is sitting among her friends and guests, dressed in white and gold and looking very much like the chief celebrant. She's glowing with beauty and pride at what she's accomplished today, making sure this wedding happens and is a glorious event. The paparazzi can't get enough of her, as they snap away, taking special shots of her gele, her designer purse, and her diamante shoes. She too smiles when she sees Rachel looking beautiful, as she descends the stairs. Her admirable gaze sends the paparazzi, like flies, to the feet of the bride.

The bride poses for a few shots on the grand stairway, and takes a special one with her sister at the bottom of the stairs. Soon, she's guided to the presence of her groom, who is seated with the chiefs and elders, ready to claim her as his wife. As she approaches, she and the congregation of aunties surrounding her sway to the drumbeat of the musicians, as they prepare for the main event.

The groom is seated in royal blue and burnt orange; the special fabric Rachel picked out for them in Dubai. After this first phase of the ceremony, she too will change into the regal garment and be paraded with her husband, as they are taken to their special loveseat as man and wife. Right now, Doug is enraptured by his bride. She's more beautiful than he has ever seen her, more glorious than he even dreamed possible. He watches, mesmerised by her dance, wanting to join in, but being compelled to follow due protocol.

The bride finally stops before the groom and the elders. The drums are silenced, and the ceremony commences with introductions and gift presentations. The father of the bride leads in prayer over the union, calling blessing and favour upon the marriage.

The ceremony continues when Rachel departs to change into her regal garment, now traditionally married to Doug.

***

Mr and Mrs Douglas Olumide leave the presence of the chiefs and elders and are presented before the people as husband and wife. Their parade starts from the main lounge to the decorated compound outside, where many of their guests are seated in anticipation. The wedding cake and loveseat share a special canopy, and a traditional band plays celebration songs under the sun.

Rachel and Doug dance like the happy bride and groom that they are. They are joined by some family, friends, and well-wishers. The jubilant and generous spray them with money, which the bridal train collect into bags to give to the bride at the end of the celebrations. Rachel does not feel the five-inch heels on her feet, nor the tight gele on her head. She's overwhelmed with joy as she celebrates her marriage to Doug.

When they finally settle in their loveseat, after their parade, Rachel begins to feel the pain of looking beautiful. But it doesn't fade her smile nor dull her laughter. She poses continually for photographs with her family, friends, and her husband.

After signing the marriage certificate, the time comes to cut the cake. The Eden family are called first to pose, behind the large wedding cake, with the bride and groom. Then the

Olumides and Folushos take their photos with their son and his new wife. After a group photo involving all the families, the couple is left standing to take some special shots, before the countdown to cut the cake begins.

When directed by the MC, the crowd spells out J E S U S, and the couple holds down the knife together. It's a beautiful photo as they both smile for the camera.

CHAPTER NINETEEN

"Dearly Beloved, we are gathered here, in the presence of God Almighty, to celebrate the union of our Brother, Douglas Olumide, and our Sister, Rachel Eden…"

Rachel stands before the minister and beside her chosen groom, in a long, white, satin gown, a veil over her face, white gloves on her hands and golden sandals on her feet. Today, there are no nerves, because the marriage is already done traditionally. The white wedding is a formality and the reception to follow, a grand celebration of what took place two days ago. Today, her Christian brothers and sisters become witnesses to the truth that she chose Doug to be her husband, just as he chose her to be his lawfully wedded wife.

There's a great turn out among their friends, colleagues, family, and church members. There are also many media houses represented, to capture the newsworthy event of Chief Ejiro Russell Eden's first daughter's marriage. The church hall is adequately decorated, but the bright colours of the aso'ebi many of the guests opted to buy, makes every picture a sensational delight.

The minister prompts the bride and groom to exchange their vows and exchange rings. The ceremony progresses. Time is given for anyone who knows of a lawful reason why

THE NAIVE WIFE: RACHEL'S CHOICE

they should not be joined in marriage to speak up, and the room is held in silence. Moments later, the minister pronounces the titles and duties of husband and wife on the couple, to the cheer of all.

Following the church wedding ceremony, the couple and the congregation sit to hear a word from the officiating minister.

"Douglas and Rachel, you are now married. You have become one, and your life together in knit in a way that it would be devastating to both of you if you were to later choose to separate. The Lord has commanded, and the wise will heed; *"what God has joined together, let not Man separate!"*

"Douglas, as the husband, your entire duty to your wife is to love her. You have been given an example in Christ Jesus. Seeing how He laid down His life for the Church, you too are to lay down your life for your wife. Consider her as your own body; respect her, cherish her, adorn her, nurture her, protect her. In any way you ought to love yourself, love your wife even more.

"Rachel, as the wife, trust your husband, as a humble follower should. Honour him with your respect and submission, and uphold him with your love. He is not a perfect man nor leader like Jesus, but support him with faith and obedience so that he will grow in confidence *and* competence. If you honour your husband's leadership, you have fulfilled your duty as his wife and helper.

"To the both of you, I remind you to serve one another and take the lower position. If you continually humble yourself, you will be lifted up. But if you exalt yourself or lord control over each other, you will surely be humbled. In the Kingdom of Heaven, the greatest is the least. The one who serves is truly the anointed master. So, if there is any competition, let it be in your service to one another.

"To all the brethren who have come to witness this solemn, but joyful, ceremony, I bid you to watch over your brother and sister with love. They have been sent out to accomplish the purpose of God, to shine the light of His love upon a dark world. See to it that you do not stand as tempter nor devourer, accuser nor tail-bearer to their union. Lend yourselves to God to offer them guidance and a good example to follow, so that they too will be faithful to the high calling of marriage. May the Lord help us all, amen!"

"Amen!" the congregation agrees.

***

Rachel and Doug enjoy a luxury drive in Chief Eden's Lexus limousine to the wedding reception in Lekki Phase 1. They remain seated in their special car, as the wedding party prepare to dance into the reception hall, which is filled to the brim with invited guests and family. Some friends come to speak with the couple, rejoicing over them anew and asking if they need anything.

Rachel doesn't need anything. She can't wait to get out of the car and dance her heart out. She's smiling from ear to ear because she knows she looks beautiful. Her dress is magnificent and flattering. Her hair is divine, and her face is glowing like an angel. Only that she's beginning to sweat, and has to pat her face gently with a face towel.

"Here, let me help you," Doug says, as he takes the towel from her, carefully attacking the areas that have too much shine.

"Thanks, baby," she says.

"You're welcome. You look *amazing*, wifey!"

"And you look dashing, hubby!"

They both giggle at the new nicknames they've given each other.

***

At last, it's time for the wedding party to make their grand entrance into the wedding reception. Bose comes to assist Rachel out of her seat, and help her to keep her dress from dragging on the sandy ground. Rachel holds her bouquet proudly, as she makes her way to the entrance, where Doug is laughing with his groomsmen.

The song they'd chosen to dance to is now playing, and with a bang, the party starts. D'Banj sings jubilantly, "*Omo, you don make me fall in love…*" The six bridesmaids are accompanied by six groomsmen into the hall, as they dance their way to the centre, where there's a dance floor laid out.

Rachel and Doug follow behind, dancing freely to the music; smiling, laughing and greeting friends along the way. The crowd cheers them on and their moves get more daring and creative. The TV screens, stationed all across the hall, capture the views that many guests cannot otherwise see. They all watch the latest wedded couple in Lagos dance their way into marital bliss.

When they finally get to the dance floor, the gloves are off, figuratively and literally! Rachel can't stand the heat of the gloves she's been wearing since the church service and quickly hands them to one of her bridesmaids, as she continues to dance, winding and grinding to the music. Doug loves it. He takes the cue and lets the music take control. Guests leave their seats to spray the happy couple with money; some even spray dollars. And the bride and groom just keep on dancing for their fans.

***

Rachel and Doug are seated in their garden-themed loveseat, as the MC takes control of the event. The dance-off is over. It's time to announce and appreciate all the excellencies that took time out of their busy schedules to honour Chief and Mrs Eden and their in-laws today. Laughter erupts through the hall, as the MC is joined by a comedian, and their energies are combustible. Rachel and Doug are giggling along at the pair.

Some friends and well-wishers approach their loveseat to congratulate them and wish them a happy married life. Some just want them to know they came, as they sneak off soon after, and others want the couple to be aware of the gifts they brought. They each stop to take photographs with the couple, before making their way back to their seats.

Rachel is pleased to see Dongjap approaching them. He is accompanied by a pretty woman, and she's happy knowing that he has moved on and is in a relationship now. Doug is also happy to see them, and Dongjap introduces his girlfriend, Tina.

"Congratulations, again!" he says, after they have taken a quick photo together.

Rachel lets out a sigh. She feels a little sad that Ejike couldn't come and celebrate with them. She wonders how he's doing and hopes that he's happy with his move to the US.

"You okay?" Doug turns to her, noticing her mood change.

She smiles reassuringly. "I'm great!"

He affectionately rubs her thigh as they smile at each other. Before long, they are laughing again at something the comedian says.

***

It's time for the Father/Daughter and the Mother/Son dance. Rachel and Doug both get back on the dance floor to slow dance with their parents. After their dance, Chief Eden hands his daughter over to her husband for their first official slow dance as a married couple.

Doug takes Rachel in his arms, and she rests her head on his broad chest, as they sway to their chosen wedding song; "I Swear" by All-4-One. Rachel listens to the lyrics and feels pure happiness, her hope sure that she and Doug are ready to face the days ahead together. She smiles up at him, and he's looking down at her. Their lips meet in a sweet kiss, and they continue to kiss as they dance. All around them, their friends take photos and videos, but they don't leave the dance floor until the music comes to a complete end.

"Wow! That was intense!" the MC says, pretending to wipe sweat from his brow.

"E be like say he think say she be food! They never chop?! Abeg, waiter, carry food put for table, before person turn to carnivore!" the comedian jokes. Doug and Rachel giggle as they remain on the dance floor, being joined by their friends.

"E don do, e don do! E no be cake-cutting time?" the comedian continues.

"Yes, oh! Doug and Rachel, it's time to cut your cake. We too, we wan chop!" the MC says, his hand guiding the couple to stand behind their cake and cut it.

"Oya, where the knife dey?" the comedian asks. "E be like say these people no dey hear, oh! We dey hungry for here!"

"Relax, nau... Food dey plenty for here," the MC retorts. "Okay, there is a knife! Praise the Lord!"

"Hallelujah!" the comedian leads the guests to respond, as they all laugh at the two hosts.

Rachel and Doug stand again, before another grand cake, to cut and share it with their family and friends. This cake has six layers, and each is lined with fresh roses, following the garden-themed wedding. At the MC's prompting, they spell out the word L O V E and cut their cake, cameras flashing in their eyes.

***

After feeding each other cake, as is the custom, the couple sit down to more marriage advice from a pastor and friend to their parents, who has graced the event for this cause. The pastor leads the assembly in more prayer for the couple and pronounces blessings on their marriage. They both affirm "Amen" to every point. Rachel hesitates when the pastor begins to prophesy that she will have twins and triplets in Jesus name! *Noooo, I don't want that many kids, oh...* But the cheerful assembly shout a louder AMEN!!!

As the ceremony wraps up, the time comes for Rachel to throw her bouquet. Her girlfriends and some of the single ladies invited gather to catch it. Rachel winks at Bose, who's standing in the middle of the crowd, directly behind her. She releases her bouquet and turns to see the scramble to get a hold of it. Alas, Bose doesn't catch it, but at least it's one of her friends and colleague, Seun. Seun celebrates by jumping up and down, and Rachel laughs, pleased for her.

Afterwards, Rachel leaves Doug to freshen up, change into her second dress, and touch up her lipstick, which has dulled since their passionate kiss on the dance floor. On her way back from changing, she meets Ryan and his fiancée. They are seated with Richard, Rochelle, and Ekene. Cassie is a blonde-haired, blue-eyed Caucasian, who's stunningly beautiful. If she hadn't been sufficiently glammed up as the bride, Rachel might have been shy to stand next to the beauty.

"Awww, I love your dress!" Cassie beams at Rachel, who grins happily. Her second dress is simply to die for. She's banking on Doug's adoration too when he sees her in it.

"Thank you! And thanks for coming all the way. I hope you're having a great time…"

"Yes! Your brother's a good host," Cassie smiles at Ryan.

Ryan stands to hugs Rachel. "Congrats, sis! You look fantastic!" She beams.

Ekene also stands and hugs her. "I think we'll be going soon, Rache."

"Sure, I understand." She goes around to hug Rochelle. "We should see tomorrow before you leave." Rochelle nods.

Richard smiles at her. He's distracted with a woman he's talking to. Rachel smiles back and waves at him, before moving on.

As she moves through the reception hall, she notices that the room has thinned, as the official ceremonies have concluded. The live band is still playing classic African songs, and the guests are drinking and enjoying small chops, ice cream and other treats. Most of those remaining are the younger folks, who are planning to dance the night away. She goes up to her girlfriends and bridesmaids, and they all swoon over her dress.

She's pleasantly surprised when she feels thick arms wrap around her from her back. She turns her head to see Doug. He has a strange look on his face as he beholds her from above.

"Babe, this your dress… E dey do me strong tin, oh!" he whispers.

Rachel bursts into giggles! It's sure to be a fun and wild night tonight, she imagines. Seductively, she winds up against her husband, and he squeezes her tight.

The DJ takes over the sound system, and old school jams set the tone for some late-night jamming. Naughty By Nature leads the train with their "Jamboree" song. All the youths familiar with the song get out on the dance floor to rock it.

As usual, Rachel and Doug have a great time out together. Rachel can't see that changing in the foreseeable future. They make a great couple. She made the right choice.

CHAPTER TWENTY

The newly wedded couple are driven to a hotel in Ikoyi, where they will spend their first night as a married couple, before going on their honeymoon. The executive suite that Chief and Mrs Eden booked for them is indeed prestigious, and Rachel marvels as they look around at the facilities. She's particularly impressed by the shower and bathroom, which is very spacious and luxurious. She can't wait to get in the massive tub with Doug, now that they have no limitations in their intimacy.

"What do you think? Isn't it great?" she asks Doug.

"Hmmm… It's nice."

Rachel turns to look at him, surprised that he doesn't agree that the place is amazing. He has opened the minibar in the lounge area and is looking at a bottle of red wine. He carries it into their bedroom and places it by his side of the bed.

"I think I want to take a shower," Rachel says, unbuckling her high-heeled shoes, which she has managed to walk in, stand on, and dance with all day. They were pretty comfortable, as they have thick straps and wide bases on the heels. Definitely a good buy, she thinks, smiling as she admires them again. "You want to join," she flirts.

"No, not now. Thanks," he says, sitting on the bed and checking messages on his phone.

She sighs. "Okay."

After her shower, she changes into one of the sexy lingerie she bought while in Dubai, especially for her wedding night. She thought she would be wrecked after the long day but she, surprisingly, still has lots of energy. She comes out in it and poses by the door of the bathroom for Doug.

He looks up from his phone. "Hmmm… Come over here…"

She beams and goes over to the king-sized bed. Doug puts his phone away and begins to undress himself. Rachel helps him, getting excited about their first time. It's not exactly her first time. She knows what to expect, and looking at the size of the man she'd chosen to marry, she expects to be impressed by his girth below too.

When he's sufficiently undressed, he kisses her lips passionately, and Rachel savours his tongue in her mouth. He lays her on her back and takes off her sexy knickers. He tries to penetrate her in the next move, but she's surprised to discover that he isn't sufficiently hard to succeed. They make out a bit longer, and he tries again. But things just don't work out as expected, and only one of them goes to bed satisfied.

***

The next day, they travel to their honeymoon destination to enjoy two weeks stay at the luxurious Labadi Beach Hotel, Accra. It's an all-expense paid trip, covered by the Edens, for which Rachel and Doug are very appreciative. Chief Eden has also informed them that he has a home he's built for them, as their wedding gift, and it should be all ready by the time they return. Rachel's indeed overjoyed, as she hadn't anticipated such support and generosity. She naively assumed she'd build a life with Doug from the ground up and, in a way, had been excited at the prospect of that. But this was so much better!

Rachel's looking around at the scenery, as the sun sets in a new country. The air feels different, almost fresher. The landscape is beautiful and the buildings, fascinating. They drive into the hotel grounds, and she's blown away. It's even more beautiful than the pictures she'd seen on the Internet, when browsing ideal holiday destinations. She needed somewhere for which visas wouldn't be hard to obtain nor take long to process. Ghana just made sense, and she'd fallen in love with the hotel when she'd seen the pictures.

"Wow, it's so beautiful," she marvels.

Doug is looking around smiling. He loves it too. They are shown to their suite, which isn't quite as exquisite as the one they spent last night in but is still very lovely, with everything they need to be comfortable and happy for the next two weeks. The best part is the amazing view of the Atlantic Ocean and the Labadi Pleasure Beach, just a walk away.

She's looking out of the balcony, when she feels Doug behind her. He wraps his arms around her, and she turns around in his embrace. They kiss happily. They are married now; Rachel thinks and sighs.

"What do you want to do?" she asks, looking at him with longing. Since last night, they haven't tried to have sex again, and she's eager to enjoy that experience with him.

"Let's look around, get some food, and then come back and chill," Doug suggests.

"Sounds great," she says.

***

After their tour of the grounds, they settle at the restaurant to have their dinner. Night has now fallen, and the resort looks even more beautiful in the dark. The swimming pool, just beside the restaurant, is an alluring blue, beneath a star-lit sky. Rachel feels like she could go for a swim, but Doug is looking like he needs to rest. They'll swim tomorrow, she decides.

They enjoy a meal together and talk about all the things they'd like to do during their stay in Ghana. Rachel is keen to visit the Aburi Botanical Gardens, and they agree to go the following day. Doug also suggests a tour of the city, which should give them more ideas about the places to visit in Accra. Rachel thinks it's a great idea.

After dinner, they enjoy the scenery, while sipping fine wine. They also spend some minutes engrossed in their phones, before deciding to retire to their bedroom for the night. Rachel takes the initiative to run a bath for them, while Doug flicks through the channels on the TV. He finds that there is not a great deal of options, but he leaves it on a news channel, as he prefers the background noise to silence.

"The bath is ready," Rachel announces.

"Alright… Coming."

Rachel gets into the tub and is immediately relieved by the heat of the water and the effect of the bath salts she'd added. Doug soon joins her, and they have fun bathing each other. They try to get intimate in the tub, but it's not working out in reality as Rachel has imagined it many times. They decide to relocate to the bed to finish what they started.

Tonight, penetration is successful but pleasure is still not on the table for Rachel. She can't get over the pain and endures the few minutes Doug continues to thrust, until he's satisfied. She can't help the tears of disappointment that fall. But at least, it's getting better.

Afterwards, they cuddle and sleep in each other's arms.

***

Rachel is not discouraged and continues to try to attain some sort of climatic sexual experience with Doug. They try different positions and locations, and sex gets more enjoyable, even though the pain remains. Through it all, their sexual intimacy grows, and they get more comfortable with each other.

They enjoy the tours and visit many places of interest. They enjoy dining at restaurants, watching films at the cinema, and window shopping at the mall because they do not have much money to spend on things. They also enjoy the amenities available at their hotel, like the spa, the gym, and the pool. By the time their two weeks is over, they have gone everywhere tourists go in Accra, and even made day trips to other cities.

The day has arrived for the lovers to return home. They have really enjoyed their honeymoon. Rachel's favourite memory is of their dinner by the pool, where a jazz band entertained the guests with acoustic music. She thought it was so romantic, and the ocean breeze that blew endlessly felt sensational against her bare neck and shoulders. She'll definitely miss the hotel and looks forward to visiting it again soon.

Their flight to Lagos leaves in two hours, and they are now on their way to the airport. Rachel is resting on Doug's chest, at the back of the taxi. He's stroking her arm affectionately and watching the road, appreciating the sites one last time. It's been an amazing time away, and now he's returning home to his own house, somewhere on the island; that much he is sure of. He also has a meeting scheduled with Chief Eden's friend on Wednesday, about a managerial position in his company. He smiles. *This is the life.*

***

Three Months Later…

RACHEL'S DAIRY
October 1st, 2014.
Dear Diary,
It's been a while since I wrote to you. I've just never been good at journaling, but I'm going to try because I feel I need

someone to talk to and somewhere I can pour out all the emotion I'm feeling.

I met a man last year who I felt I really connected with. He was rather persistent and seemed to really get me. We started dating about a year ago actually, just days after my 32nd birthday, and by Christmas, he proposed. Honestly, I thought it was all moving too fast and wanted a long engagement so that I could get to know him more and really feel that we were in love.

Well, with the advice of my parents, we had a short engagement and got married on June 21st. So, I've been married to Doug, that's his name, for three and a half months now, and I suppose we're happy. But I still don't really think that we are in love, the way I always wanted to be with my husband. I don't want to say I made a mistake, because I really thought I was being led by God, but something does not seem right…

I've seen things, I've heard things, and I feel like I can't trust my husband. The other day, a friend of mine told me that she saw another woman in his car and they looked 'chummy', and she was very sure it's him. I didn't want to believe her, but when we were home watching TV last night, someone kept sending him messages, and I got curious and checked them. It was a girl or young lady, who had taken pictures of herself in his car and was sending them to him.

Of course, I confronted him about it, and he assured me that it was completely innocent. I had to tell him that I didn't like it at all, and he needs to keep boundaries to protect our marriage. I don't know if I got through to him. Honestly, he didn't seem moved, but I don't want to worry about that now…

The thing is, I'm pregnant. I suspected I was a few days ago and confirmed today at the clinic. I'm happy about it. I want this baby, but I can't help feeling like I'm not in the marriage I thought I was. We're just not the way we used to be. We don't really talk like that, and he definitely doesn't show the same interest in me nor give his attention like he used to. I'm sure it's not uncommon, so I don't want to say he's changed, but…

Anyway, I'm an aunty now. Rochelle got married last August and had a baby girl two months ago in America. They are still there and doing really well. They're supposed to be coming back this weekend.

Well, I just thought I should get my thoughts down, and maybe I'll get a better understanding and feel better about the things going on in my life. I hope to write soon. Later!

TO BE CONTINUED.

ABOUT THE AUTHOR

Hi, I am Ufuomaee. I am a writer, blogger, and Christian fiction author. I tell stories to help young people make the right choice before marriage and deal with challenges that often arise during and after. I also use parables and poetry to teach about God's love. When I'm not writing or working, I love to watch action movies and romcoms on Netflix. I also love reading romantic and inspiring books by other amazing authors, which I review on my blog, www.ufuomaee.blog.

CONNECT WITH ME

BECOME A PATRON: www.patreon.com/ufuomaee
AUTHOR PAGE: www.amazon.com/author/ufuomaee
FOLLOW ON FACEBOOK: @ufuomaeedotcom
TWITTER: @UfuomaeeB
INSTAGRAM: @ufuomaee
WEBSITE: www.ufuomaee.org
BLOG: blog.ufuomaee.org
EMAIL: me@ufuomaee.com

Check out my full catalogue of books at
books.ufuomaee.org